D1168985

WHAT'S IMPORTANT IS FEELING

ALSO BY ADAM WILSON

Flatscreen

HARPER PERENNIAL

NEW YORK • LONDON • TORONTO • SYDNEY • NEW DELHI • AUCKLAND

WHAT'S IMPORTANT IS FEELING

STORIES

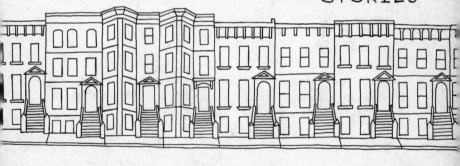

ADAM WILSON

HARPER  PERENNIAL

These stories previously appeared, in slightly different form, in the following publications: "Things I Had" in *Meridian*, "December Boys Got It Bad" in *Tin House*, "We Close Our Eyes" in *Washington Square Review*, "Tell Me" in *The Literary Review*, "Sluts at Heart" in *The Coffin Factory* (as "That Underlying Want"), "America Is Me and Andy" in *Word Riot*, "What's Important Is Feeling" in *The Paris Review* and *The Best American Short Stories 2012*, "The Porchies" in *Promised Lands: New Jewish American Fiction on Longing and Belonging*, and "Milligrams" in *Cousin Corinne's Reminder*.

HarperCollins books may be purchased for educational, business, or sales promotional use. For information please e-mail the Special Markets Department at SPsales@harpercollins.com.

FIRST EDITION

Designed by Michael Correy

Library of Congress Cataloging-in-Publication Data is available upon request.

ISBN 978-0-06-228478-5

14 15 16 17 18   OV/RRD   10 9 8 7 6 5 4 3 2 1

FOR MY PARENTS

As if we held in the heavens of our arms
not cherishable things, but only the strength
it takes to leave home and then go back again.
—DENIS JOHNSON, "ENOUGH"

CONTENTS

WHAT'S
IMPORTANT
IS
FEELING

SOFT THUNDER

No one knows who slept with her first. Besides, sleep isn't the right word. What we did: pressed lips to closed lips, tried to slip in some tongue; buried her beneath us on carpeted floors and futon mattresses; fumbled for buckles; felt her dry skin against our sweat-wet hands; said, "Don't cry"; wiped tears with our T-shirts; kept on because she said, "Don't stop."

I met Kendra at Norm's, the retro-chic diner where I worked weekends bussing tables. This was the end of junior year. Norm's had a jukebox straight from *SkyMall* that played the same golden oldies all shift long, and a special sauce—mayo plus Tabasco—you could add on for a dollar, get your fill of fat and spice. The manager's name was Wyatt, but he went by Madonna. Around close he'd unplug the juke, turn up the kitchen stereo, and lip-sync "Like a Virgin" with a mop for a mic, while the rest of us hustled to count out and clean.

Wyatt was the first out gay I ever met, a tube-tanned blond who both smoked cigarettes and chewed Nicorette. He took personal calls on the takeout phone, ducking behind the counter to answer, whispering to what I imagined was a variety of lovers, the covert homosexuals hiding out in my hometown. The markings of a clandestine existence were enough to make him my hero. Plus, he bought me beer and smokes without double charging like Tim Qwan from school, who had a fake ID and a sense of enterprise.

"Big Daddy," Wyatt called me in his lispy southern drawl. "Big Daddy, baby, unplug that juke for me, old man."

"Yes, boss," I said, and saluted. "Right away, captain, boss man, sir."

It was early to close, but Norm's was pretty empty. Just a couple in the corner drinking decaf, dreading home. Wyatt slipped me some Nicorette. I was new to tobacco, and the gum gave me a low buzz, like an ice cream headache that sinks down to your stomach in a sickly, nasal drip. Wyatt's mixtape came over the PA: drum machine and synths, Michael Jackson in falsetto. Wyatt pogoed the serving floor. He slapped Claire, the lifer waitress, on a veiny, muscled thigh.

"The way you make me feel!" Wyatt sang.

"Old." Claire said. "You make me feel old, Ms. Madonna."

"Hush, now," Wyatt said. "You're as young as the last boy you opened your legs for."

"Then I must be getting on sixty," Claire deadpanned.

"Bless your heart," Wyatt said. "Bless your generous heart, Clarice."

"Jesus Christ," Claire said, and touched the cross around her neck. She was among the last of our town's Italian Catholics. They lived on the north side, by the lake. Had their own unofficial mayor, Alessandro D'Ambrosio, a nose-broke man of late middle age with half a dozen daughters and supposed ties to the North End mob. D'Ambrosio was always in the local paper, posing at christenings, serving sausage to kids on Columbus Day.

"But what you really need, Clarice, is a young stud like old man Big Daddy Benjamino here," Wyatt said, and pointed at me.

I must have been blushing ketchup red. Ernesto, the Costa Rican cook, caught a case of the giggles. The cooks were half-cocked by this hour, hoisting rum-punched plastic Coke bottles. Wyatt was grinning. He always was.

"If she's lucky," I said.

"Maybe if he puts on some weight," Claire said. "Benny, why don't you join a gym, hon? Muscle up for my obsolescence?"

I was a scrawny seventeen, shoulderless, sporting the wispy premonition of an oncoming goatee. My hair was a mop of floppy bangs, Bic-singed at the tips. Claire struck me as someone who had never been young, who from birth had been fading from unknown, prenatal glory. Wyatt himself must have been pushing forty. I didn't know how he'd landed in these suburbs, far from home, a lifer like Claire: partnerless, all but partied out.

Madonna swooped over, swept me off my feet. He pulled me onto his imaginary dance floor, roped me with an air lasso, spun me, dipped me like a lessoned bride.

For a moment I felt weightless, safe in Wyatt's ropy arms. Then I saw her.

My first impression was that Kendra looked like a doll. Her face seemed sculpted, porcelain pale, with large glassy eyes and perfect pink circles painted over her cheeks. Matte black hair hung nearly to her waist in a puff of voluminous waves. The hair probably accounted for a third of her weight. She was skinny, barely a body, just accumulated clothing on a stingy set of bones.

At seventeen we all craved D cups, skin we could sink in to take refuge from our own unmanly selves. Kendra had a different appeal. She reminded me of the chicks on MTV who thrashed among the boys, snarling jaw-clenched from the throat. Her outfit added to the image: steel-toe boots; jeans with holes in the knees; some kind of gothic, lacy bodice, a costume perhaps forged with sewing machine from an older sister's lingerie. Kendra had the expression down too, that punky sideways stare: pupils tipped to corners, mouth ambiguously pursed.

Her parents, on the other hand, were dressed in clothes too hot for June, and too formal for Norm's: woolen evening wear, the remnants of a cross-continental journey, possibly by steamboat. They looked like the peasants on the covers of the Russian novels I'd been skimming for English.

"Hello?" her father sang out in a basso-Balkan growl. "Is anybody working in here?"

It occurred to me that I was still in Wyatt's dippy embrace. He rubbed my nipple through my shirt and made a kissy face. The kitchen staff was in hysterics. Kendra looked at me and winked.

"Wyatt," I whispered.

"I don't answer to that name."

"Madonna, fine."

"Sing it to me tender, Daddy," Wyatt said, and kept on rubbing.

"Customers," I said.

She took timid bites of pancakes, a couple sips of soda. Pushed fork around plate, rolling it in syrup and then licking the tines. Her parents were animated, upset, ravenous. Her father waved his arms, stuffed a sandwich in his mouth, exclaimed something in another language. He was crying. "We'll get through this," her father kept saying. "It will all be okay."

Kendra excused herself from the table. She walked right past me on the way to the bathroom, slipped something in my pocket, and pecked me quick against the cheek. She smelled like maple syrup and a scent I couldn't place, cleaning products maybe, the faint whiff of chemical lemon.

The note said: "Leave twenty-five dollars in my locker and I won't tell anyone at school that you're a faggot. Kisses, Kendra."

Sam lived in one of the beastly mansions—built by my uncle Marion—that were uglying our town. The mansions were arranged in ovular cul-de-sacs, like linemen in huddle, lording over their lawns. The style was some kind of pseudo-Roman abomination, columned and pillared, moon white in the moonlight.

Inside, there were all the sleazy signifiers: hot tub, steam room, ten-headed shower. Sam's house had a fully stocked bar. His dad had run off with a supermarket magnate six months prior. The magnate was older, with a bleached mustache in blond relief against her upper lip. Sam's mom mostly stayed upstairs, her authority stripped, her hair in curlers. I didn't yet understand that adults could be drunks in a different way than kids could; that instead of pounding beer and taking shots they sipped vodka toward sleep, cried out to no one for the lives before their lives.

My own parents were slightly older, of a different generation of Jews—ex-hippies who'd smoked themselves silly in the sixties and now preferred a half glass of red, nothing more. They looked down on parents like Sam's, the tacky and tastelessly rich. The work ethic—it was suggested—had been weaned out of our people. We'd grown soft in luxury, aspiring Wasps toasting Bud Lights to full assimilation, while the Chinese and Indians filled our old Harvard spots. I wasn't doing much to preserve the old ways. I forged on, beer by beer, brain cell by brain cell, junior college bound.

In Sam's garage we drank from the ransacked bar and grew weed—a weakling of a plant that turned out to be male and unharvestable but looked good in Polaroids. We were drinking club soda mixed with melon liqueur. We were down to the dregs of the bar.

"A cool girl, you say?" Sam said.

Our school had a shortage of cool girls. Cool girls were girls who smoked pot and dug guitar fuzz, would skip class to take shrooms, craved indiscriminate cock. We only had one. She was Roland's older sister and wanted nothing to do with us.

"Fo shizzle," I said.

Roland just nodded. He was jaded, over everything. He'd been fucking a Canadian cousin since age twelve. Roland was good-looking and good at hockey, and people wondered why he hung out with the rest of us.

"Damn, yo," Alex said. "I'm gonna get up in that bitch." Alex was our wussiest and tried the hardest to sound tough. He wore wire-frame glasses and jeans that hung below his butt.

"I'll believe it when I see it," Sam said. He was the skeptic son of a wrecked marriage, kind of a dick.

The garage door opened to the street. We sat in lawn chairs, studied the drip of spring rain like we were in a diorama looking out. Across the cul-de-sac, lights lit empty rooms. Alex fell asleep, snored. His head hung limply, chin to chest. Sam sipped, surveyed. Roland spat. Some CD hummed: a chortling bass, the low rumble of tom drums. In the distance I heard thunder, way off to the west.

"Well, shit," Alex said, roused.

Roland lit a cigarette, blew smoke at the rest of us.

"Bring it," Sam said. "Bring the motherfucking thunder."

"Damn, bitches," Alex said. "What time is it?" He looked at his wrist but wasn't wearing a watch.

"Almost midnight," Roland said.

Alex was walking to his car when it looked like lightning struck him. He was down on the ground, shaking and twitching. It took a moment for the rest of us to realize we should run over. Alex's eyes rolled up into his head. Only the whites were visible. He looked like a hooked fish flopping in the bottom of a boat.

"Call an ambulance," I said. I'd meant to scream it, but the words had come out whispered. No one did anything. We didn't have cell phones.

"I don't want the cops here," Sam said. "What about the weed plant?"

Alex lay shaking, making gurgles and groans. His tongue slipped in and out of his mouth.

"Dude," I said, and pointed. "He's dying."

"It's fine," Sam said. "This has happened before."

Sam and Alex had known each other longest. Sam knew things about Alex that the rest of us didn't. "Give it a minute," Sam said. "He'll be fine."

We stood there getting wet. Sam checked his watch.

"What is it?" I said. "What's happening?"

"A seizure," Sam said.

"Aren't you supposed to do something with the tongue?" I said.

Roland knelt down and held Alex's wrist, steadied his head. After a second, Alex stopped shaking. His eyes rolled back around. Roland and I pulled him up so he was standing. Alex was wobbly. We tried to help, but he pushed us off. His glasses were caved in at the middle, falling off one ear.

"Damn, bitchass," Alex said, and pushed me. "You better not tell anyone about this, Ben. You and your big fucking mouth."

The lights were on when I got home, but only my sister was up. She was in her room with the door closed, the soft strum of girl folk seeping out through the crack. Trish had recently returned from freshman year of college, ten pounds overweight and in a state of psychological distress. She'd woken one morning to her boyfriend's boning moans from the other side of the room and an offer from her roommate to loosen up and join the party. Now she spent her days here: eating ice cream, holding forth to my mother on the failings of my gender. I felt like talking, like telling someone about Alex just to prove it had happened. But Trish wanted privacy, wanted nothing to do with me.

I walked through each room extinguishing lights. The lit rooms looked almost like museum displays, each impeccably vacuumed, no signs of lived life. They felt foreign in their emptiness, a world outside the world of day. Upstairs, I could see that Trish was online.

I typed, "Hey."

She typed, "What?"

I typed, "Nothing."

Kendra was the reason for the band. Sam had spied her practicing after school in the empty art room. The way he told it, she had one leg balletically propped on the windowsill. She leaned into sunlight, pushed the music from her tiny center. The sun came through her skin. In that light, Sam said, she'd looked almost translucent. "Like a lizard," Sam said. The fact that clarinet was the wrong kind of instrument was completely beside the point. The point was to get her in Sam's garage.

It was my job to approach her. I tapped her on the shoulder. She stared into her locker. There was a mirror inside there.

"Hey," I said.

Kendra didn't turn. She could see me in the mirror; I could see the left half of her face, powdered white, lashes stiff with mascara.

"You got my money?" Her face—or at least the left side of it—did not betray a sense of levity.

"Fuck your money. I ain't paying." I flashed the flirtiest smile I could muster. All around us was the zip and whiz of high school halls, lockers banging in the background.

"I guess I'll have to break your kneecaps then."

"I'm Ben," I said.

"Well, Ben, you seem like a nice guy. I'd hate to see you crippled."

"I'll take my chances. You play clarinet?"

I pointed to the case inside her locker.

"I'm Hungarian," she said. "Of course I play the clarinet."

"Of course," I said.

Then she was in Sam's garage, wearing what looked to be a bandanna tied around her tiny breasts. She fiddled with her reed, dumped spit on the cement floor. We stared.

Eventually, Sam started a drumbeat, the only one he knew. Roland's bass sounded in like a series of low moans, barely rhythmic, but bracing in their volume. I plucked an arbitrary chord. Alex's keys produced a lion's roar—the coolest sound effect on his old toy Yamaha.

"What key are we in?" Kendra asked.

"Key?" I said.

Roland shook his head, gave the bass a bit of slappity. Sam smashed at his cymbals. I noodled high up on the neck. Alex nudged a few notes from the white keys.

"We're just jamming," I said. "Just some freestyle experimental shit."

"It's shit all right," Kendra said. She blew into her instrument. Out came something that sounded like music.

"Fo shiz," Alex said.

"I told you," Sam said.

Roland nodded in approval.

"She's Hungarian," I said.

There was one song we could do, an old sixties sing-along, four chords and a chorus. I was singer by default, the only one who knew the words. It wasn't singing exactly. More like a mix of talk and scream with but the merest hint of melody. We turned the mic down low and let the music drown me out. I was okay with that. When we got to the bridge Kendra came in for a solo. The other instruments went quiet. Her clarinet was tense and trebly, flouncing up and down the scale. Dusk was coming on. The wind picked up, poured into the garage, carrying smells of cut grass and distant grilling. Kendra kept going, another eight bars. Her eyes were closed. Her body hardly moved. Just long thin fingers fingering, pinkies lifted, index tapping out the meter, thumb continuously curling. She was a virtuoso, or had maybe just taken lessons.

"Earth to Daddy," Wyatt called, hands cupped around his mouth. I'd been spacing out, writing lyrics on a napkin. The song was about Kendra, but I'd veiled her as a meerkat. I'd been watching lots of nature shows while stoned. In the song, we were lovers in captivity, trying to fuck our way to freedom. I'd managed to rhyme zookeeper with Grim Reaper. I couldn't wait to show the band.

"Work is calling, Big Daddy. No more poetry—time to wipe some tables. Dinner rush is almost here."

We were getting to the end of June. School was over. The heat brought out hibernators, folks emerging from cave-homes for oversized sundaes. I was constantly mopping the sticky floors, wiping tables, washing bucket loads of glassware. My fingers were wrinkly, suds-softened. I smelled like milk and Windex.

"Yes, boss," I said, and crumbled the paper. Wyatt wasn't gonna let me off that easy.

"Hand it over, Big Daddy, let lil' ole Madonna get a look."

He grabbed at the napkin, managed to rip off a corner.

"Never," I said, and stuffed the rest in my mouth and chewed. Claire sidled up to us, placed an arm on Wyatt's shoulder. I spit the chewed napkin in the garbage.

"What tastes so bad, Benny?" Claire asked. "That fruit plate in the kitchen? Because I think Ernesto left it out overnight. I wouldn't touch that if I were you."

"My, my, it's the bitter taste of young love," Wyatt explained. He puckered up and made smooch sounds. "Bless his beating little heart."

Kendra was waiting by my car when I got out. She looked different under streetlight, less affable, as if posing for an album cover. She stomped a cigarette, leaned up against the car.

"Here to break my kneecaps?" I asked.

"Something like that," Kendra said.

We drove through the residential areas, past Sam's and the cul-de-sacs, past Roland's apartment complex, through the north side and around the lake, out to the quiet byway that connected us with the next town over.

The area was mostly woods, the undeveloped limits of our municipality. Soon Uncle Marion would kill these trees too, build mansions, make more money from the ugly.

Kendra flipped through my CDs, found something acceptable.

"Are you tired?" she asked.

"No," I said. I wasn't. Work had worn me out, but I was eager. The long run of it—life—looked mostly unhopeful. I would go to the JC, stay on at the restaurant, siphon from my parents until they cut me off for good. But tonight was open-ended; it would be hours until sunrise.

"I'm tired," she said.

"Long day?"

"Just tired," she said. I knew enough to let it slide. Kendra turned up the music. She opened her compact but didn't apply any makeup. She studied herself.

"The thing about cars," Kendra said. "Is that you're going somewhere, but you also are already somewhere."

"Totally," I said, and took a left.

"But that place you are isn't a real place. I mean, it's moving. You haven't arrived yet."

"Right."

"I don't want to arrive," Kendra said. "I don't ever want to arrive."

"I'll need to get gas eventually," I said, an attempt at a joke. Kendra didn't laugh.

"Park somewhere," she said.

I doubled back to the women's fitness center, found a spot in the sequestered lot. It was late but the lights were on in the center, the tennis bubble lit white. Kendra and I stared at each other across the car's console.

"Hi," she said, and gave a thin smile.

I leaned in for a kiss, but Kendra pulled away.

"Not that," she said.

She opened her door, stood outside, lifted her dress over her head, and dropped her panties to the ground. Clothed only in Doc Martens and a couple of bracelets, Kendra stood with arms at her sides. My headlights were off. Kendra's black hair blended into the dark. Her body looked like a child's; the skeleton seemed uneven, south-sloping. One breast was bigger, about the size of a golf ball. The other was almost completely flat. Her bush was dark and wispy and trailed up to her belly button. Her legs and belly were bruised in places. For a moment I thought she might disappear, fade into nighttime, vanish in a slow roll of gray smoke.

She got back in the car, fit herself between my body and the steering wheel. Objects dug into us: seat belts, soda straws, empty cigarette packs. I tried to kiss her again, and this time she sort of let me. Her lips were dry. Her cheeks were wet with tears.

"We don't have to," I said. "Are you sure?"

"Shut up," Kendra said. She raised her body, lowered herself onto me. I didn't last long. My penis went flaccid. Kendra bounced up and down with increasing vigor.

"I'm soft," I whispered.

"Just shut up," she said, and kept on going.

The band was getting better. I'd written a song, not the meerkat one. It was a minor-key ballad called "Car"—the refrain: *I don't want to arrive.*

Kendra liked it. The others were indifferent, but her vote counted more than theirs. We'd secured a gig for the following weekend, playing Wyatt's July Fourth bash. The band needed a name.

"It sounds like a fart," Sam said, and tried to twirl a stick. The stick slipped from his grip and fell. "A womanly fart."

"It doesn't," I said. The name was my idea.

"Well, not like an actual fart," Sam said. "But a description of one. Like if someone asked, 'What did that fart sound like?' one might reply, 'Oh, soft thunder.'"

Roland shrugged, plucked an E string. His amp produced a low and reverbed note. I took this as a vote on my behalf.

"I like it," Kendra said. "It's retro, kind of seventies. Kind of Fleetwood Mac."

"Exactly," Sam said. "A shitty decade and a shitty band—just what we want to be!"

"I like it," Kendra said, which settled the matter.

"No dizzout," Alex said.

"Fine," Sam said. "Whatever." He picked up his drumstick, played a snare fill, silently fumed.

After practice I drove Kendra to the Bickford's out on Route 1. To get there, you had to pass this big oak where some kids were killed a few years back. They'd been speeding and lost control of the car. For a while the tree was decorated, surrounded by framed photos, drawings, flowers, notes tacked to the trunk. Now there was no memorial. Weeds grew back in around it. It was hard to remember which tree was the right one.

"Some kids died there," I said. Kendra paused a moment before responding. She inhaled deeply. I thought she was being dramatic. It's not like she knew them.

"I'm gonna die," she said.

"We all are," I said. "Everyone in the world. Everyone we've ever loved." It was something I'd heard someone say in a movie. What I wanted to say was that I'd never loved anyone, not yet, but maybe if she'd let me I would fall in love with her. I could lie on top, blanket her body.

Bickford's had that unbearably cold air-conditioning that comes from the ground and freezes your flip-flopped feet. Everyone in there was old—waitresses and patrons—life's cooling leftovers. There was a nursing home across the street, the Star of David, an unkempt drop box for Jewish seniles. Trish was always threatening to put our parents there.

Kendra and I ate in almost silence. Well, I did. She ordered chocolate-chip pancakes but didn't take a single bite.

"Not hungry?" I said, sneaking my fork into her food.

"Go ahead," she said. "I don't eat." She said it like it was supposed to be funny.

"Oh," I said. "Okay."

"It does sound like a fart," she said.

Later, entwined on my futon, after many minutes of unexplained crying, Kendra told me that as a girl growing up in Hungary, she would sneak into the living room at three in the morning to watch a show that played American music videos. She said that her whole life all she'd ever wanted was to be in a rock band, to have sex and get high and wear outrageous outfits, and that she was glad she was getting to do that now. She said she was happy. I wasn't sure what to do—what the appropriate response was—so I reached for her hand and held it. I said, "That's good."

• • •

"Drinky-pinky time!" said Wyatt, brandishing a waiter's profuse armful of plastic cups. His T-shirt said "Put a Little South in Your Mouth." The cups were filled with a fruity concoction, heavy on vodka, garnished with floating gummy bears. I was on my third. The party was in full swing. A sign said "Welcome Homos and Hookers!!!" The crowd consisted of the former costumed as the latter. According to Wyatt, it was the summer of leather short shorts.

Wyatt lived in a ranch-style condo with a couple other gay guys. The décor was Hawaiian, apropos of nothing. Leis and grass skirts were handed out at the entrance, and the yard was lit with tiki lamps. We were on the porch, a perfect little outdoor stage. Ernesto wore three leis around his thick neck. He slugged his drink, crushed the empty punch cup in his fingers.

"These fruitcakes sure know how to party!" Ernesto said. He had an arm around Wyatt.

"Oh, you're bad," Wyatt said, and flicked Ernesto's puffy cheek. My friends watched in awe, unsure whether to be embarrassed or amused. We were setting up our amps, waiting for Kendra to arrive.

"The thing about these fruitcakes," Ernesto explained, "is they know a lot of sexy ladies."

"True dat," Alex said.

"Depends on your definition of sexy," Sam said.

Claire was in a group of women with perms and press-on nails. They smoked long cigarettes, and their laughter led to coughing. The gays were teaching them dance moves. The girls giggled as they tried to two-step in stilettos. I'd never seen Claire out of work, gussied up. Maybe it was the booze and mood light, but she looked younger for once, face softened, less severe.

Even my sister was at the party. I'd invited her by e-mail but didn't think she'd bother. Trish had hardly been out of the house since her return. She'd arrived alone, looking tentative, too pale for summer. But the gays had welcomed her into their fold, fed her tequila shots, commiserated about her ex.

"Oh, that sorry little man-child," said Wyatt, and waved a finger. "He gon get what he got coming."

Trish was nearly too drunk to stand. "I'm a fag hag!" she screamed in my ear. "Benny, I'm a fag hag!"

"Awesome," I said. Soft Thunder were the only ones not having fun. We scanned the crowd for Kendra. I hadn't heard from her in days.

"I saw her Wednesday," Sam said. "We went and saw *Titanic*."

"Really?" I said. "*Titanic*?"

"Just the two of you?" Alex said.

"Yeah," Sam said, "Just us two."

"I took her bowling," Alex said. "I think that was Thursday."

"Bowling?" I said.

"Bowling's dope, yo. Don't fuck with bowling."

"I saw her yesterday," said Roland.

"Okay, boys," Wyatt interrupted. "Let's get rolling before this crowd gets any rowdier."

The conversation would wait. There were bigger things at hand. Sam sat behind his drum kit. Alex strapped on an

American flag bandana he'd bought for the occasion. He took off his T-shirt, waved it over his head, tossed it into the audience, played the lion's roar on his keyboard. A few people clapped. Wyatt killed the stereo. I tapped my finger on the mic.

We opened with the sixties sing-along, vamping on the chorus for a good ten minutes before seguing into "Car." Our third and final song was a surprise for Wyatt. We'd been practicing an awkward cover of "Like a Virgin." The crowd gasped, applauded. Wyatt appeared onstage wearing nothing but jockey shorts. I moved away from the mic to let Madonna do his thing.

It would have been triumphant if Kendra hadn't then appeared. She'd snuck onto the stage and was suddenly standing next to me. Her head was completely hairless.

There's something unsettling about a shaven head. Maybe it's that you can really see the skull, the shape of it, all its lumps and juttings, skin stretched tautly over bone. So little separates our brains from the world.

Kendra blew out the melody on her un-amped clarinet. No one could hear it, but she played on. The rest of us— Roland, Alex, and myself—circled in on her, a pathetic pack of teen wolves. Even Sam's drum kit seemed to gravitate toward her.

When the song ended we were pulling at her arms and saying "Baby" and "Kendra" and "K." She broke out of our huddle and escaped into the party. We tried to chase after her but were plugged into our amps.

"I've been," I said. "I mean, she and I have been—you know?"

"You?" Sam said.

He swung at me. I ducked and he missed, tripping over some cables. Alex charged us both, windmilling with a look of pure insanity, knocking everyone over. Except Roland—he shook his head. Wyatt helped me up.

"Where'd she go?" I said.

"Big Daddy," Wyatt said. There was wisdom in his tone. "Oh, Big Daddy."

Someone turned the stereo back on. ABBA blew in and the dance lawn exploded. It looked as though the dancers were jumping, trying desperately to launch. Fireworks went off over the lake. They were the cheap kind of bottle rockets that flare low with white sparks and then fall into the water.

When I found Kendra, she was in the neighbor's yard, openmouthed, Trish's tongue stuck down her throat. They groped like babies at each other's breasts. Trish had her shirt off. She was swimming in sweat.

I ran, leaving my car and equipment. The fireworks were still going; they sounded like gunshots, aimed at me. I was drunk and hadn't run since I'd quit soccer sophomore year. After a couple minutes I tired out. I stood in the middle of the street with my hands on my knees, head hung between legs, crying, vomiting. I was a few miles from home.

We didn't see Kendra at all during chemo. She was with Roland now; we got word through him. Roland was a rock, the right man for the job. Everyone agreed. He stayed evenings at the Brigham until visiting was over. After, he'd sometimes stop by Sam's garage, but he never stuck around more than a few minutes. We'd offer bong hits and beers, but he refused. Said he just wanted to give us the update. Said he was tired.

The rest of us were at it full force. We drank every night, smoked until we couldn't stand. It wasn't long until we got onto other stuff—stealing pills from Sam's mom, buying Oxy and blow from this friend of Roland's sister. I got fired from Norm's for showing up high, sold my guitar to stay that way.

The chemo killed more cancer than her doctors had expected. A marrow donor was found. According to Roland, the operation went well. The cancer had been excavated, and I wondered what was left; there had been so little body to begin with.

One two a.m. I heard rocks against my window. I hadn't been sleeping—not that night or any others. I would stay up online in chat rooms with pseudonymous strangers, saying the most awful things I could imagine—really sick things I wouldn't wish on anyone. The words flowed from my fingers in manic bursts. I could type like this for hours. I felt possessed, as if there were some other me controlling my emotions, sending all this vitriol into the world.

When I opened the window I was expecting Kendra. I don't know why—I had a feeling. I thought she would be down there, hair grown back in, looking just like that night when I'd first seen her at the restaurant. We would apologize and she would kiss me and from then on we would never leave each other's sides.

I came out in pajama pants. Summer had passed and it was getting on fall. The wind hit my face like cold fingers. Roland looked me up and down. I could feel that I was shaking.

"She wants to see you," he said. It pained him to say it.

"Now?" I said.

"They're moving. Back to Hungary."

"Why does she want to see me?"

Roland stared at me for a long minute. "You're an idiot," he said. "I always thought you were the smart one, but you're an idiot."

"I can't," I said, and went back inside.

I work for my uncle Marion now. We've built a new town where the woods used to be. We bulldozed all those houses on the lake. Not us personally, but the people who work for us. I sit in an air-conditioned office playing fantasy sports. From my office I can see our new skyline, shimmering silver, blotting out the stars.

Sometimes I eat at Norm's. Wyatt's gone—who knows where—but Claire is still around, still the same. The last time I saw the others was at Alex's memorial. We stood in his parents' kitchen, making small talk, looking at old photos. There were photos of the four of us—one from that night at Wyatt's. We have our arms around each other. We look so young. It was only a few years ago.

Alex seized in his sleep, choked on his tongue. Sometimes in bed, I grab hold of my wife and pretend that she's Alex. I put my hand to her mouth and imagine reaching in, past tonsils and esophagus, elbow-deep, down to his intestines. Alex trembles. I make a fist around his innards. I'm waiting for the moment when it all goes still.

THE LONG IN-BETWEEN

In August of 2006, during Israel's relentless bombing of Lebanon, and days after Mel Gibson said his piece about the Jews, I came to New York City to live with a woman who had once been my college professor.

Her name was Elizabeth, and she was staying, for the summer, in a SoHo loft previously occupied by an internationally famous daytime talk-show host. The Host had since moved one flight up to the building's penthouse, where he threw lavish parties, audible through the floorboards, a weekly reminder of New York's immutable social infrastructure. No matter how high you climbed, there would always be someone above you.

I knew none of this when I arrived on the Fung Wah bus from Boston. It was a hot day, and humid. The sky was purple-gray, clouds swollen with coming rain. My hair was a mess. My bra clasp dug into my spine.

I dragged my suitcase from the subway, eyeing the women on lunch break whom I'd come here to become: interns in bubble skirts tapping furiously at cell phones, their legs moving in long, deliberate strides. They appeared to be members of a similar but distinctly different species. A taller species.

The elevator opened directly into the apartment. It was an oblong, open space decorated in a series of large abstract paintings accented in gold leaf, and ugly. The furniture looked imported from a Palm Beach condo: white shag area rug with matching throw pillows on white leather love seats and recliners. The walls were cream colored, or crème colored, according to Elizabeth, who occasionally affected a Pan-European patois. The other walls were windows. From certain angles you could see across Greene Street into the Apple Store. A kitchen emerged at the end of the room, complete with two industrial sinks whose gleaming hoses wrapped themselves like long bracelets around the spouts.

I was not particularly impressed. I'd grown up middle class in an upper-class suburb of Boston and had spent countless hours in friends' McMansions just as tastelessly gaudy as this Prince Street apartment. The décor signified a brand of generic wealth that I had come to find provincial.

Elizabeth appeared from behind the fridge.

"Darling, you're here," she said. "Welcome. Isn't this place hideous?"

Elizabeth walked on tiptoe; she still fancied herself a dancer, though she'd quit ballet in college. She wore a terry-cloth robe that showed off striated thighs and taut, toned calves. She was three inches taller, but otherwise we looked almost the same: flat chests, no hips, prominent cheekbones, "penetrative" brown eyes, Ashkenazi noses, and pale skin caked with foundation. It was a look that had failed me through high school and most of college, but I had high hopes for my new life among the sun-fearing fashionistas. Androgyny was back after an overdue hiatus.

Elizabeth, almost twenty years my senior, was the product of previous boom times for heroin chic. She'd spent the better part of the nineties complementing the look with an actual needle stuck in her arm. After rehab, she'd managed to buckle down and finish her thesis, a sunless tract on AIDS and the American death drive. The published version had earned her a small following in certain academic circles. Now she carried herself with a jaded self-confidence that attracted men and women alike—but mostly men, and mostly gay—and that I did my best to emulate.

During my four years of college I had developed what is sometimes called a girl-crush—though the term sounds too cutesy for what I felt—on Elizabeth. I'd taken her class on late capitalism (the syllabus was divided between Edward Said and Judith Butler) in the second semester of my freshman year. By semester's end I had already copied her hairstyle (straightened black bangs), clothing style (gothic airline stewardess), and eating style (S.S.S.—soup, salad, sashimi), and was finding excuses to stop by her office on an almost daily basis.

Elizabeth was new to Boston—she'd done her graduate work at Columbia—and seemed appreciative of both the company and worship. I saw her as the epitome of urbanity, and the embodiment of an academic idyll that otherwise existed only in past tense novels by nostalgic baby boomers. Elizabeth and I played out this campus fantasy, smoking imported Gauloises on the library steps and discussing all relevant isms. But mostly we talked about the men in our lives, whom we referred to as our *dudefriends*.

"Dudefriend thinks it's his life's work to sperm up my eggs," said Elizabeth, once. "If only we were lesbians."

"If only," I said, unsure what she meant. Was the implication that we would be a lesbian couple, or just a couple of lesbians?

"I mean, I'm not one of those overpopulation people, or worse, the oh-so-magnanimous doomers who don't want to subject a future generation to blah blah blah. But what happens when my son is molested by his math teacher?"

"Isn't that a cross-that-bridge-when-you-get-there sort of thing?"

"Oh, he'll definitely get molested," said Elizabeth. "The question is whether to uphold the traditions of our rape-shaming society by telling him his body has been traumatized, or refrain from comment and hope he remembers it fondly, some kind of passionate hug session from the man who taught him Boolean algebra."

"What kind of school are you imagining this is?"

"School of hard knocks," said Elizabeth.

When she decided to sabbatical in Manhattan, it seemed natural that I tag along. I was, by then, two years out of college, with no life goal except the vague intention to move to New York as soon as I could afford it. Elizabeth was able to secure me an internship at an ad agency run by an old family friend, so long as I promised to maintain ironic distance from the industry's consumerist credo, in much the same way that Elizabeth "ironically" bought dresses at Barneys.

She led me to a small room behind the kitchen. The floor was stacked with books and printouts. There was no desk, just a coffee table, couch, and mounted plasma television, unplugged. A week-old *Times* was open on the table. The photo showed a bombed-out building in Beirut. A shirtless man lay injured in the rubble, trapped beneath fallen pipes. Another man tried to lift him out by the arm, but the injured man appeared limp and immobile, content where he was.

"My office," said Elizabeth. She cleared space so we could sit. We lit cigarettes. Elizabeth ashed on the couch.

"My cousin's," she declared with a wave. "Or his for now at least. He bought it for eight, wants to sell it for ten. Old story. And I get to squat here until fall when the market's meant to change. The art and furniture are rented, by the way. I did my best to dissuade him."

I'd heard of this cousin, an I-banker. Elizabeth liked to brag about the non-penetrative experiments they'd engaged in as adolescents in Pittsburgh. The Cousin was tall and handsome, and still felt guilty about these encounters, which he remembered as being only semi-consensual. Elizabeth remembered things differently—in her version, *she* was the aggressor—but she liked the power position his guilt placed her in. For years he'd been paying off Elizabeth's Amex.

Elizabeth caught me scanning the *Times*.

"Hideous," she said. "Just hideous. Women and children they're killing. Innocents. It makes me sick. And the macho Republican Zionists like my cousin cheering them on."

The last part irked her most. Two things Elizabeth hated were Zionism and machismo, though she'd flirted with the former on kibbutz after college ("Yitzhak Rabin and pharmaceutical-grade ecstasy, darling—those were different times") and the latter was a trait she proudly manifested. I do not mean to suggest that Elizabeth's sympathy for Lebanese civilians was insincere, but something about the word *hideous*—the same adjective she'd used to describe the apartment's art—made me wonder if it wasn't all theory for her, some kind of ideological chess match unrelated to actual suffering.

"It's terrible," I said, and hesitated, resisting a defense of what I knew was indefensible. Israel was a sore subject between us. I'd been indoctrinated early, and there were feelings from my upbringing I had trouble abandoning. Members of my own family had been exiled from Europe, shipped to Palestine for refuge while their parents were murdered. Besides, the Arab treatment of women and homosexuals didn't seem to mesh with the radical queer feminism we both espoused.

"You're right," I said. "Horrible." Which it was. Israel was behaving horribly with its showy display of firepower, raining bombs over Beirut as if it were a video game. I'd said so to my father when he'd defended the attacks, ranting at the dinner table about Hezbollah, spearing a chunklet of chicken on his fork and waving it for agonizing minutes while he continued to talk. "They want to destroy us," he'd said, but it was he, with his hate-filled eyes and four-pronged flesh flag, who appeared bent on destruction. He and the young Israeli soldiers I'd seen photographed shirtless on the Internet, holding Uzis in perfect hip-hop posture.

At home, it was easy to argue with my archaic, conservative parents, but out in the world I fought urges to defend their worldview, to fight my leftist friends who seemed to stick up for every minority group except the Jews. There was general agreement that assimilation had happened and anti-Semitism in America was a thing of the past, but I couldn't shake the sense that this dismissal was its own anti-Semitism, or an excuse for it. Jews were the new Wasps: privileged, powerful, perfect targets for blame.

I sniffed my armpit.

"Take a shower, darling," said Elizabeth. "The bathroom's something to believe."

The fete was held so I might meet prospective suitors. I'd recently broken ties with my dudefriend, Clarke, who'd taken a prestigious gig gofering for the House's only out-gay congressman. *Suitors* was the word Elizabeth used. *Fete* was also her word, though it was only a dinner party. The real fete was upstairs, at the Host's apartment. His bass shook and rattled the glass table, making music with our tumblers.

Elizabeth leaned into Mike, her on-off, surprisingly all-American dudefriend. The others disdained him and baited him, he of the strong jaw and aggressive heterosexuality. According to Elizabeth, Mike had once been a star PhD candidate in sociology at Yale, but a car accident had rendered him partially brain damaged. He occasionally showed flashes of past brilliance, blurting full-formed ideas after hours of silence, but most of the time Mike fumbled his words, failing to articulate what was there on the tip of his tongue, tantalizingly out of reach. He was also always drunk. Mike was a happy drunk and treated me with warmth. Elizabeth's friends brought out the worst in him.

"Stop, please," Mike said, but Nikil kept on talking.

"Michael," said Nikil. "I am not, as it were, defending Melvin Gibson. I am simply pointing out that, if the situation were reversed—if Mr. Gibson had slurred against Arabs or homosexuals—then no one would be quite so up in arms."

Mike pressed tumbler to forehead and let out a sigh. We'd been on the subject for most of the evening, but Nikil couldn't let go. Mo leaned into Nikil and squeezed his partner's elbow.

"It's no use," said Mo, shaking his shiny, shaven head. "He's never going to understand." They spoke of Mike like he wasn't there. It occurred to me that Mike, a protestant from Chicago, was the only member of the ethnic majority in our group.

"Well, if you won't defend him, then I will," said Elizabeth. I thought she was talking about Mike. Elizabeth rose from her seat, raised her tumbler.

"Mel Gibson had every right to say what he said," said Elizabeth. "It's about time someone did."

"*Salut*," said Nikil, and they clinked drinks. Elizabeth wiggled her butt a little bit.

"If the situation were reversed, then wouldn't Mel Gibson *be* the Jewish one?" said Suitor #1, a brunette named Brian Feldstein whom I disliked immensely.

Feldstein was attractive enough, with clean teeth, hazel eyes, and the kind of the cock-clipping skinny jeans that were just coming into style. What annoyed me was his closeness to Elizabeth. He'd graduated a year ahead of me, and was, by all accounts, her first and truest protégé, a whip-smart artist of the sneer and bon mot, in whose shadow I stayed. Besides, I thought he was an asshole. In class he'd always cut down my comments, and at parties he alternated between ignoring me and acting overly familiar, draping an arm over my shoulder and calling me "kid." I considered Feldstein my nemesis. Not that I'd say so to Elizabeth. There was an erotic element to his idolatry that Elizabeth enjoyed and that I couldn't quite provide. I sensed he saw me as some kind of consolation prize. I solaced myself by imaging Feldstein masturbating in the dark, cradling his pathetic penis, resigned to the fact that he would never fuck either of us.

"We mustn't speak in hypotheticals," said Nikil, who always spoke in hypotheticals. He himself had been a protégé, along with Elizabeth, of the great Said. "We must approach the reality of the situation, which is this: the *Israelites* invaded Palestine, brought about apartheid, and *enjoy* the careless killing of Muslim women and children. To phrase it any other way would be to euphemize, anesthetize, soften the blow. We cannot share sympathy with this murderous regime. We cannot let tribal allegiances get in the way of reason."

Elizabeth listened intently, still standing, prepped for another *salut*. I wanted to point out that Palestine and Lebanon were two entirely different countries. Mike refilled his scotch and drank it down in a long gulp without grimacing. Tonight was more of the same—the things he put up with for Elizabeth's love. Or "*love*," as she often reminded us, fingers raised in fangish air quotes. Feldstein placed a hand on my knee. Mo looked at Nikil and said, "Lighten up," and Nikil's face broke into a boyish grin, and soon everyone was laughing.

"Sorry," said Nikil. "I'm so used to trying to fire up my students that it carries over into dinner party zealotry. Jesus, this is good scotch."

Suitor #2 lit a joint and passed it to Nikil. When their fingers touched, #2—another old friend of Elizabeth's from grad school—leaned into Nikil and noogied his head.

"The picture of ethnic harmony," said Elizabeth. "If only you two were the leaders of nations."

The evening went as planned. After ten minutes of #2's valiant but futile cunnilingus, he stroked my hair and said he understood. He'd seen my face; he knew it wasn't easy to leave the tribe. "Nikil knows he's a hypocrite. He would be stoned to death in Pakistan. The best thing that ever happened to him was being sent to that boy's school in London."

The word *lover* is ridiculous—perhaps even redonkulous— and it speaks to my state of generational denial that I referred to #2 as my lover, and refused to acknowledge that *redonkulous* was a word. That fall, when I was sharing a place in Greenpoint with Jenny and the Piñata Artist, I used the word *redonkulous* to describe, among other things: piñata art, Elizabeth, the Prince Street apartment, and Mr. #2 himself.

My lover was exactly twice my age, and from Omaha, but he lived like a British bachelor, surviving on Heinz beans, bodega tomatoes, and Earl Grey tea. He owned neither mop nor broom, and was constantly reshaping his redonkulous goatee.

The situation wasn't exactly what I had in mind, but Elizabeth seemed so happy about the match, and I liked the way he knew what I was going to say before I said it, and that he read poetry as well as theory, and his furry gut, which I found refreshing after years of envying Clarke's smooth six-pack. Elizabeth said it was always a good idea to date someone uglier than yourself, though she'd broken her own rule with the objectively hot Mike.

#2 had a poorly self-assembled Ikea bed frame, so we spent most nights that week on an air mattress at Elizabeth's—the Cousin had rented decorative furniture to display to potential buyers, but not beds. We shared a spare room the Host used for stashing his children when they'd visited from L.A. The rooms had not been repainted, and ours bore a safari mural on all four walls. Giraffes, monkeys, and lions watched over as we screwed and talked and slept.

The sex had improved considerably since Elizabeth and I had bought matching vibrators. I could get off in mere minutes if I used it while he entered from behind. For her part, Elizabeth said Mike refused to incorporate the object out of masculine insecurity. She said it like she was impressed.

In the mornings I would head to my internship, dressed in clothes from Elizabeth's closet, plus a pair of heels from Barneys that she'd bought me on the Amex and that raised me to an appropriate height for a SoHo intern.

The work was tedious and brainless—light administrative stuff and the maintenance of a couple Excel spreadsheets—but I was happy there, bitching with the other interns about the idiocy of our bosses and of print advertising in general. None of us planned to stay past summer. Print was dead, digital was here, and these old-fashioned agencies would be razed to make way for start-ups that better appreciated our web-heavy résumés.

I went along with this talk, though I was privately a print nostalgic, fantasizing about using the gig as a gateway to glossy magazines. Anything seemed possible. The others were from Reno, Gainesville, and Iowa City, and I came to understand that the SoHo aliens I'd initially found threatening were only posers like me, that in fact all of *real* New York was itself a simulacrum of the somehow *realer* New York of our Hollywood-assisted imaginations.

Happy hour was upon us. Jenny said, "Ugh, I hate my arms," code meaning either "Compliment my arms" or "Criticize a part of your own body in solidarity." She was a fellow intern, an FIT grad from Seattle with an upturned Irish nose, prominent American breasts, straight blond hair, and impeccable fashion sense. Jenny complained ad infinitum but registered these complaints in the knowingly jocular tone of one who understands the relative triviality of her issues. I could tell she thought I took myself too seriously.

"My neck makes me look like a bird," I said, and waited for someone to disagree. No one disagreed. We sipped vodka tonics, vodka-tinis, and marga-Tito's, which were like margaritas, but with Tito's brand vodka instead of tequila, plus a splash of Red Bull.

"Your guy's in the news again," said Jenny.

"What guy?" I imagined #2 on the front page of the *Post*, led away in handcuffs by campus security. A girl points an accusatory finger. She's wrapped in a blanket and looks like a less birdlike me.

"The talk-show host. Dude's been getting crunk since the breakup. Plowing through B-listers. He's supposedly throwing these parties every night. It's super sad. You gotta get your skinny ass up there."

"Perhaps," I said, and checked my cell. I was supposed to meet Elizabeth, Mike, and #2 for dinner in twenty minutes.

"Can't you ditch?" said Jenny.

"Elizabeth would kill me. She had to pull strings to get the reservation."

"Or at least meet up later? Party tonight at Aaron's. Maybe find a boy your own age, sucka."

"Sorry," I said. "Maybe next time." I pounded my Tito's and left a twenty on the table.

The line at the restaurant spilled onto the street. Mike stood apart from us, smoking, giving off a moody vibe.

"What's his deal?" I asked Elizabeth.

"Probably his period," she said.

#2 let out a giggle, but I felt bad for Mike. He and Elizabeth got along in private, but she treated him terribly around other people. My favorite night so far was Sunday, when the three of us had watched a movie on Elizabeth's laptop. The film was plotless and opaque. Instead of paying attention I'd focused on Mike, whose body lay beside mine, Elizabeth's head in his lap. Mike's fingers curled around her bony biceps, closing so thumb met fingertips. I could tell that Mike too had lost interest in the film—only Elizabeth followed the action on-screen—but he wasn't bored. He looked perfectly peaceful stroking her hair with one hand and her arm with the other, the weight of their bodies sagging the air mattress, making my side rise up like a small, cresting wave.

At dinner, when the plates had been cleared, Elizabeth made an announcement.

"I've decided to write a screenplay," she said. "Get out of academia once and for all."

"Get out of academia?" said #2. "That's devil talk, lady. Blasphemy. Universities are the last safe places for ideas in this capitalist oligarchy."

Universities were also the last safe places for #2. They accommodated his perpetual adolescence—the drinking and fanciful facial hair and impressing girls like me—and he took offense at Elizabeth's insinuation that his kingdom was a ghetto. That Elizabeth had tenure made it more annoying. #2 adjuncted at Baruch and City College, mostly freshman comp. He blamed his failure to rise on the fact that Jews weren't the beneficiaries of affirmative action. This was a good thing for society, he made a point of pointing out, but bad luck for him as an individual.

"Academia," said Elizabeth, "is just so academic."

"So what's the screenplay about?" I asked, horrified. Why wasn't I privy to this information before she'd made the announcement? Why hadn't she asked me to collaborate?

"Postmodern incest," said Elizabeth.

"As opposed to the other kinds of incest?" said #2.

"As opposed to bullshit," said Elizabeth.

"This should be good." Mike's tone was sarcastic. He'd finished four bourbons during dinner. Mike slumped in his chair, pulled at his open collar.

"I don't follow," said #2.

"It's the last taboo," said Elizabeth. "The film is about a brother and sister who announce themselves as a romantic unit. Their parents don't understand. Their friends don't understand. Even you all at this table, my closest friends, my most"—air quotes—"*enlightened* friends, look at me like I'm sick for uttering the word."

Mike didn't look at her like she was sick; he looked at her like he was sad. He had a pained wrinkle between his eyebrows that reminded me, for a moment, of the Lebanese man lying injured in the rubble.

"Stop talking," Mike said.

"No, I want to hear this," said #2. "Please enlighten us, Elizabeth."

"The shrink thinks the girl has Stockholm syndrome. That it all leads back to childhood trauma. Truth is, brother and sister are incredibly attractive, and they want each other. They"—air quotes—"*love* each other. The love"—air quotes—"*that dare not speak its name.*"

"And what about kids?" said Mike. "What about the . . . the . . ." His arm made a circling motion.

"Genetics?" I said.

"Genetics," Mike repeated. "What about the goddamn genetics?"

"They don't plan to have children. They see themselves— their lifestyle, really—as the end of the evolutionary line. They are the last generation. It's a de-evolution, a return to amoeba sexuality, the final frontier for humans."

Mike made a fart sound with his mouth.

"I think what Mike means," I said, trying to diffuse the tension and make myself indispensable, "is that it seems unbelievable for them to be American characters. But what if you made them German? Could that work? I think that would make a lot of sense."

"But I still don't understand what it's *about*," said #2.

"She wants to fuck her cousin," said Mike. "That's what it's about."

"And that makes it postmodern?"

"I slept with my cousin years ago," said Elizabeth. "That has nothing to do with it."

"You said you only did second base," said Mike.

"And that doesn't *count*? Is that what you're saying? That the sex act is only complete once the man has come to climax?"

"It's a joke to you," said Mike. "Everything's a joke."

"Darling," said Elizabeth. "I'm dreadfully serious."

"You're ruining . . . ," said Mike. "You're ruining . . . and you're so fucking noncha . . . noncha . . ."

"Nonchalant," I said, though I'd lost the thread.

"Nonchalant," said Mike. "So fucking nonchalant. You're ruining your life."

"By writing a screenplay?"

"You know why," said Mike.

Elizabeth barred her arms in an X across her body. "This is not your decision," she said.

In bed I asked #2 why he'd never dated Elizabeth. I'd assumed he wasn't up to her intellectual standards.

"Are you kidding? She's a psycho."

"Eccentric."

"Psycho. You know she was in the nuthouse, right?"

"You mean rehab. For heroin."

"That JAP's never shot heroin in her life. Maybe she snorted it once or twice."

"Don't call her that. It's an ethic slur."

"But I'm Jewish."

"That makes it worse," I said. I rolled over, checked my cell. There was a picture text from Jenny. She posed beside a pyramid of White Castle burgers. A tattooed dude leaned toward the pyramid with his mouth wide open. The way they'd shot it made it seem like he had a giant mouth, big enough to fit all the burgers at once. Jenny looked like she was laughing.

"You don't like me much," said #2. "Do you?"

"No," I said. "I guess I don't."

The roof overlooked Manhattan from across the river. A film crew was set up on the street below. A fifty-foot crane lit the neighborhood, sharing long beams of light like a small, near sun, giving the city in the distance a surreal mystic shimmer, as if it weren't there at all but were only a hologram sprung forth from the crane's godly glow. Jenny held her phone over the edge to snap a photo. The photo came out blurry, black with a dot of white light at its center. "Ill," said Jenny.

There were no more dudefriends or lovers. Elizabeth had ignored Mike's calls for three days. #2 hadn't even texted.

Jenny took my arm. We crossed the roof and then descended the ladder back into the party. A dozen donkey piñatas hung by tinsel from the ceiling. The piñatas were decorated with Polaroids of battered women. Every hour, the artist would ceremoniously smash one with a Wiffle bat, spilling an assortment of loose pills onto the partygoers. A group sat Indian style on the floor, sifting for Adderall among the Advil and CVS-brand antihistamine. The installation was called *Mules*.

Some dancers made a circle at the room's center. Jenny said, "I love this song," and pulled us in. Her style of dancing approximated jumping. She bounced farther toward the ceiling with each upbeat, mouthed the words. It looked like Jenny was speaking in tongues, perhaps in prayer to the great lord of gravity, asking to be lifted, weightless, above us all.

Jenny's eyes were closed. The other dancers looked around as they jangled, trying to match each other's moves, or gauge the aptitude of their own. A dude made exaggerated air-humps in my direction, buffering against rebuff by pretending to be joking. I pictured Mike on the dance floor, pre-accident. In my head he was confident, fleet-footed. He wore a fedora, tap shoes, a white tuxedo.

I thought about leaving the party and showing up at his apartment. Mike in a bathrobe and day-old stubble, pleasantly surprised when he opened the door. We would not say a word. He would open the robe, and I would press my body against his, head to heart. He would close the robe around us.

I knew I was not someone who would show up at Mike's

apartment. Not out of loyalty, but because I was afraid. At some point, I let the air-humper hump my leg.

The clinic was just around the corner. The magazines were either in Spanish or stupid, so I stared at the TV while I waited for Elizabeth. The UN had urged both states to ceasefire, but Hezbollah refused to stop sending rockets and Israel refused to stop dropping bombs. CNN's aerial camera circled over northern Lebanon, zooming in and out on devastated areas. From above, the region looked like a beat-up map, with certain sections so heavily creased and worn they'd become literal gray areas, topographical erasures.

In a few days, the current conflict would end, but I remember thinking, as I sat in the Planned Parenthood waiting room, that both parties were too stubborn and hateful to ever truly change, and so were condemned to an eternal cycle of murder and mourning, with occasional respites in between. Sometimes the respites were brief—a month, a year—but occasionally there would come a long in-between, long enough for the people to forget their grief and enjoy the prevailing peace. And I remember thinking that this state of being—the long in-between—was the best life had to offer.

On the walk to the clinic I'd asked Elizabeth if she was sure she wanted to go through with it. I'd seen enough movies to know I was supposed to ask.

"I'm forty-one," said Elizabeth.

"That's not too old," I said, though I wasn't certain of the science.

"I'm not against procreation," she said. "But I'm not sure I'm in favor of it either."

Two weeks later I will come home to find Elizabeth fucking my nemesis Brian Feldstein on the floor. He will be on top, arms clenching her neck in a not so gentle strangle. Elizabeth will moan, "Don't stop." When Brian sees me, he will turn and say, "Sup?" but he won't stop strangle-fucking, and Elizabeth won't even notice that I'm there. Shaking with anger, I will get back in the elevator, ride up to the penthouse, and trail a group of young women into the Host's apartment. The room will be filled with people I vaguely recognize, and the Host will weave among these people, stopping for handshakes and back-claps before moving on to the next group. The Host won't stop smiling, as if any change in expression might transform him into another, lesser being. When he approaches me, I will lean in and kiss his cheek as if I know him. His breath will smell of cough drops. His hand will grace my hip. A blogger will snap a photo from across the room, and in the morning I will be referred to as "Mystery Woman." The photo will make it look as though he's blushing at something I've said. Jenny and my other coworkers will ask for details, and I will tell them I don't kiss and tell, but say it in such a way—slightly smirking, one eyebrow raised—as to imply that, yes, perhaps I am not so innocent as they might have imagined.

That afternoon, Elizabeth will come into the kitchen and ask if I am angry at her. I'll lie and say I'm not angry, because I have no real right to be angry. Elizabeth will say, "Well, I'm starving," and eat peanut butter from the jar with a plastic spoon. She'll say, "Don't you get it?" and I'll say, "Get what?" and she'll say, "I did it ironically. The whole thing was ironic."

When we got back from the clinic it was already evening. The Apple Store's sign lit the street, opulent white, iconic apple frozen in its bitten state.

Elizabeth plugged in the TV. There weren't any channels, just fuzz. "Shit," she said. "I never called Time Warner."

The fuzz was antiquated, analog, a remnant of another era. Elizabeth left the TV on. She laid her head in my lap.

"I have you," she said. "You're mine."

I took a long, deep breath. The A/C was cool against my neck. I wrapped a strand of Elizabeth's hair around my finger.

"I'm yours," I said.

THINGS I HAD

For S.R.

My grandfather was an old queen, and when he was dying he would grab me through my pants and try to make it hard. He had Alzheimer's and called me Sam, and sometimes I let him because it wasn't his fault and I liked the attention.

There was a tenderness in the way his fingers moved—up and down like slow typing—that I've yet to find in any lover, a word I hate; it implies love, a condition absent from my life, though I've replaced it with the companionship of late-night television.

The problem with love is that I had it for my wife, but also for the one I was cheating with. Both were Latina, young, beautiful. One broke things—vases, wineglasses—the other cleaned up the mess (she was the maid). What I had was nostalgia for the things I'd never had. What I also had was money, which counts more when you're older.

The thing with my grandfather started in the new house, which was not so different from the old house, except it was in a different state, one where the heat crept under your skin and lived in the space between your bones and your veins. Jane and I were at a school meant for Catholics. Our mother told us that after making the sign of the cross we should wipe over it with our palms in order to erase it. She was an old-school Jew torn between her fear of gentiles and her desire to get us into good colleges. St. Anne's of the Divine was Miami's best, and my father had to pull strings to get us enrolled.

As it turned out, half the students were Jews, also the children of string-pullers: textile magnates, software moguls, commercial real estate tycoons. The other half were the Cubano elite out of Coral Gables. The girls wore skirts hiked up so you could see the inward slant between the fall-off of their ass cheeks and their paler backs of knees.

In the cafeteria, Jane sat with her new friends and I was left alone, at the end of a long dining table, removed from the flirtations and legs, crossed and uncrossed, ad infinitum.

I mainly watched Celia Escarole, the light-skinned, dark-eyed Cuban Jew (Jewban) who smelled like an ultra-earthly combination of oranges and baby powder. I liked the way she fit in with her crowd, content in the middle, content to let her eyes wander. She didn't pay attention in class either, just played her click-pens like castanets and tapped her boots against the tile.

My grandfather taught me all I know about seduction, the way you start out slow, hands grazing, smiles short and repeating like blinking eyes. He didn't say much, only "Sam," in a way that barely involved his mouth. His fingers were wrinkled and felt like recently bathed skin.

The thing my grandfather didn't teach me was how to start conversations. This was problematic; in high school, introductions are necessary. And though I hoped that by sitting alone—head in a book I wasn't reading—I radiated new-kid mystique, in actuality no one looked at me.

It was probably a good thing that no one looked at me. My boners came and went like the billboard ads I watched through the tinted window of our town car, the one my father had hired for Jane and me, complete with driver, just until we got our licenses.

We moved slowly, gliding beneath palm trees, watching bikinied skateboarders weave between cars. Our driver's name was Luis, and he played Little Havana on the radio at a volume slightly lower than the sound of his hum over the music. Jane sat in her corner doing homework with a felt-tipped pen in girl-perfect freehand (she was no lefty like me, all smudged ink and oddly angled letters).

Luis also drove our grandfather and hated him because of communism—Grandpa was double pink, card-carrying. That's how he met Sam. I know because he once asked me "Remember how we met?" When I said no, he took his thumb and rubbed it over my index and middle fingers, said, "Washington, DC, 1954, Joe McCarthy in our rearview. Bill Weiss's party, that Elvis Presley record, which one was it?"

"*Blue Suede Shoes*," I said, and he nodded. When he told these stories I tried to act like I remembered.

Once I asked Maria if she remembered how we met.

"I was your maid, stupid."

"But when did you first have that feeling?"

"When you leaned over and rubbed your *pinga* on my ass while I was dusting under the coffee table."

I come from a line of failed husbands. Grandpa had an excuse. His chemistry was XY to XY. My father was simply an asshole, a cheater. My mother knew but didn't care, or cared but didn't have anywhere else to go.

I guess that makes me an asshole too.

I'm not sure if my mother was a good wife. She mostly shopped and prayed. She'd never been religious, but in Miami she went to temple every Saturday. She spent the rest of the week touring the South Beach boutiques.

Jane got a different gene. Her kids are beach beautiful, born into California. Daniel, her husband, eats low-carb in the Google cafeteria. We speak every few months. How are the kids? Daniel rides a Segway! Andrea Solomon is divorced, you know? She invites me for holidays, but I don't go. She's still mad about Bianca.

"You loved her," she says.

If I loved anyone it was Celia. First I had to get her attention. Since I was shy and terrified of females who weren't my sister, my method involved staring at her for an entire class in the hope that she would turn around and that we would "accidentally" make eye contact. The plan was foiled almost immediately when Celia did notice me, raised her hand, and said, very flatly, "Andrew Stronifer is staring at me."

It was a bittersweet moment—she knew my name!— but it was mostly bitter. The class laughed the way they laughed at geeks and nerds, which meant I was a geek, because I wasn't smart enough to be a nerd.

After school, Grandpa was the only one home. My mother should have been there, but she was out buying shoes or makeup or staring sadly at the ocean in new shoes and new makeup.

Jane and I both looked like our mother. We shared her build: all bones, no booty.

Not many boys liked Jane. She was a wallflower who hadn't grown into her face. It was strange being twins. If there was such a thing as a male wallflower I hoped that I was one. I felt like a part of the wall. Sometimes I felt like a flower, though I wanted to be something more manly than a flower.

Grandpa was a flower, and now he was wilting. He would be dead soon, and our secret would be erased. I imagined that when he died my body's memory of his fingers would lift easily, like lox from wax paper, leaving only oily residue.

Grandpa lived above the garage in a small alcove that also had a bathroom and a room filled with items: files, sweaters, an exercise bike. These items had been accumulating dust in our old house in Boston, and we'd brought them to maintain a level of continuity.

He sat up in bed, facing the television. The Lakers were playing the Knicks.

"Beautiful," he said.

"Beautiful," I repeated. Grandpa turned to look at me. It was his nonrecognition face, different from his recognition face and his déjà vu face.

"Who are you?" he said. He wore flannel pajamas and was sweating.

"I'm Sam," I said.

"You're not Sam."

Some days he knew I wasn't Sam.

Before Sam died, Jane and I would go for weekends to their house in Vermont. Sam would walk with us through the woods, squeezing our elbows with his small hands. The two of them would spend mornings in bed, and Jane and I would climb in, watch television, bring them orange juice. I imagined their lives together in sepia-tinted montage: swirling strings carrying them hand-holding through fields of daises; across supermarket aisles with one in the cart and the other gleefully pushing; beneath an awning avoiding rain, Sam holding an unfolded newspaper over young Grandpa's head. At the end of the montage the music becomes somber, the piano trills, the timpani beats a slow pulse. We see a hospital bed: now occupied, now empty. There is Sam's gravestone. There is Grandpa in this bed, Sam's pictures still in boxes, me lingering in the doorway.

"Then I'm your grandson," I said.

"I don't have a grandson."

I looked out the window, saw a branched bird trapped in sunbeam.

"You'll be dead soon," I said, half to myself, still looking out the window.

"Who are you?" Grandpa said again.

"You're old," I said, and left the room.

In my own room, I put on the Cuban station and lay in bed with the lights off. I shut the curtains but sun holograms came in from the sides. The DJ didn't play slow ones, just the tick-tick shakers with their long vowels and drums that sounded like chattering teeth. I couldn't decide if the songs were replacements for sex or preparations for it. I couldn't sleep; all I wanted was sleep.

Sleep is different for teenagers, more restorative. Now when I dream, my dreams are on the surface; when I wake I only rise inches. In sleep I can still feel the window breeze.

My family had stopped eating as a family. Dad went out with clients, and mom drank health shakes or white wine. Jane had friends and ate with them in her room or at their houses. I had become partial to ramen noodles, and Grandpa liked them too. There wasn't much to clean up. We sat on the couch watching basketball. I didn't care about the game, but basketball placated Grandpa. Maybe he liked the muscular bodies. Maybe it was televised timelessness. Watching the game with dinner, he knew who I was, said, "Andrew," "Thank you," "Your mother was such a happy girl." After our noodles I lay in his lap and he stroked my hair.

Jane showed up sometime after eleven.

"Stop staring at me," she said.

I gave her my *fuck you* eyes, the ones I'd been practicing in the mirror. She sat down next to me on the couch.

"It's bullshit," I said.

"Everything's bullshit," she said.

"Grandpa's asleep," I said.

"Mom," Jane said.

"And Dad," I said.

"Out," Jane said.

I wanted her to sit with me, let TV make us children. Instead I said, "Florida sucks my ass hair," and Jane went upstairs.

When Dad came home he was stumbling, but not too bad. His shirt was open to the third button. He'd recently acquired a thick gold chain with a Star of David the size of a throwing star. He wasn't religious. I think he wore it the way gangsters wear crosses, with a mix of false humility and messiah complex. He passed me with a nod and headed to the fridge. He removed the leftover cake, shoved it in his mouth with his hands. I turned off the TV so I could watch him in the reflection of the blank screen.

"You're getting fat," I said.

"What?" His mouth was full. I stood up and walked into the kitchenette, stuck a finger in the cake, licked off the frosting.

Dad swallowed. "Don't you have homework?" he said.

"I did it."

"Good kid," he said.

"Good cake?"

"That's what I said," he said. "Good cake."

The next day at school I walked the halls with my head down.

"Stop staring at me," someone said.

"Andrew Stronifer is staring at me," someone else said.

Class was no refuge. When Ms. Castillo said, "Andrew," I banged my head against the table. When Mr. Trund said, "Come to the board and try this equation," I stood hunched, chalk in hand, and wrote the number 666 next to the equals sign. They sent me to Father Gutierrez for counseling.

His office was simple, adorned only with hanging rosary beads and a portrait of Mary cradling her young child. Soft jazz played in the background, a trumpet moving in short bursts, a clinking piano. I sat across from the priest. He nodded at me as though he understood, knew God's world was a difficult one to navigate. I shut my eyes.

"How are you?" Father Gutierrez said.

"I'm Jewish," I said.

There was a different counselor for Jewish kids, a social worker named Javier whose office was lined with science-fiction books and posters from *Star Trek* conventions. He had shag carpet eyebrows and miniature hands, and instead of talking about my family he lent me books with intricately designed covers featuring slutty space-babes and men whose heads were half robot.

I saw Javier after school on Tuesdays. Afterwards, instead of being picked up by Luis, who had already driven Jane home, I caught the number seven bus in town, riding it out of the Grove and back to Coral Gables. I liked the smell of the bus, and I liked the people on it who didn't look up. My parents would have flipped if they knew I was taking the bus, but they weren't paying attention to me. They hadn't mentioned the increasing length of my hair, or the way I talked back in mumbles.

Summer became summer which became summer. There were no seasons, just heat and air-conditioning. Technically, it was almost Christmas.

One day while I waited for the bus with crossed arms to cover my armpit stains, someone called me from behind a tree.

"Hey, Triple Six," the voice said. I kept my head down.

"Don't worry, Triple Six, it's cool." There were two of them, lanky and pube-faced, peeking out. I walked over.

"Quick, hit this," one of them said, and handed me the remnants of a joint. I'd never smoked pot before, but only because I'd never been offered it. I took the joint and held it to my mouth.

"You gotta inhale," the other said. He was taller and pockmarked. I'd seen him around school, squirreling down the halls. I tried to push the smoke down and coughed.

"Quiet," Squirrel Boy said. "We'll get busted." I passed the joint to the other guy, who I'd never seen before. His uniform shirt was unbuttoned to reveal a white T-shirt with Charles Manson's face on it.

"Celia Escarole is a cunt fork," he said. He had a man's voice, almost Russian sounding it was so deep.

"What's a cunt fork?" I said.

"You know," Squirrel said. "A johnson scraper."

"A toothed twat," Deep Voice said.

"Oh," I said. I was trying to figure out if I could feel the weed. We each took another puff and then Squirrel put out the joint with his foot.

"Squirrel Boy," I said.

"Who's Squirrel Boy?"

"You," I said. "You're Squirrel Boy."

"Triple Six is totally lit."

"Am I?"

We walked across the bridge. A jogging bodybuilder almost knocked me over.

"What a pec-tard," Squirrel said. These were my people, I thought. They had words for things I'd wanted to name.

Back home, I lay on the couch. Jane and her friend Cressida were doing homework at the table. Cressida had wire-rimmed specs and braces, but she was pretty.

I was staring at her. Cressida didn't notice, but Jane did.

"Go check on Grandpa," she said to me.

"He's fine," I said. Jane raised her eyebrows, and I went upstairs.

Grandpa lay in bed shirtless, over the blankets, crying. His room smelled like urine, and his pajama pants were soaked through. He kept saying "I," repeating it, as if attempting to resume agency over his body.

"It's okay," I said. I took a hand—I didn't want to get too close, to invade his space—and held it the way an infant reaches out and acquaints herself with an extended finger. I removed his pants slowly, careful not to touch, to impose on his vulnerability. I took a towel from his bathroom and wiped the damp skin on his legs and on his penis.

"It's okay," I said. "It's just Sam. Everything will be okay."

I gave him a fresh set of underwear, covered him with a blanket, crawled in next to him. I wiped the tears from his cheek with my thumb, kissed his unshaven face, ran a finger through his hair.

He looked at me like he didn't know me but knew he needed my help.

"It's just Sam," I said. Grandpa moved toward me and kissed my lips. He didn't kiss aggressively, assuredly. More like someone going in for a first kiss, without expected result.

I didn't kiss back. His lips were dry. "Sam," he said. He rubbed my shoulders, wrapped his arms around my body. He rested his chin on my shoulder, calm now. He put his fingers below the waistband of my boxers. He didn't rub my penis, just held it in his hand, not for long, just for a moment, as if, by holding it, he were transferring some kind of energy, some kind of thank-you.

Then it was Chanukah. We had a menorah, but no one bothered to plug it in. I was rolling with Squirrel and Deep, sucking down jays, wearing sunglasses. Squirrel played the guitar. He didn't know how to tune it, but he could make loud fuzz and hold a cigarette between the strings. Mostly they came to my house. We'd hang on the porch and talk shit about the shitheads at school. Jane and Cress were sometimes there. I'd started calling her Cress in my head because I liked the way it sounded, like watercress. Squirrel liked her big lips because they were good for sucking dick.

"Hello, ladies," Squirrel said. "Care to join us?"

Jane fingered her protractor, turned the page. "Fuck off," she said. Cress smiled.

It was still warm outside. My mother never came home and busted us. Christmas break was in a week, but first there was the Christmas dance. Squirrel, Deep, and I weren't going, or we were going to egg it, or we were going to steal vodka from Squirrel's dad's liquor cabinet and show up plastered and vomit on jocks. We'd get thrown out of school and sent to public school to be with real people, ones who understood us, girls who liked good music.

Jane was going to the dance. Richie Cohen had asked her. I wasn't going to act all protective brother. I'd seen him in the halls; his ears were bigger than his face.

"He's a nice guy" was all Jane said. I'm sure he was a nice guy.

"You going?" Jane asked. It was late night; we were watching *The Late Show*. I wasn't stoned for the first time in a while, and I was lying there thinking about how much better it was being stoned.

"Whatever," I said.

"You should go."

"I said whatever."

"I know someone who would go with you."

"Shut up."

"Though I don't know why she'd want to, considering how lame you are."

"I wouldn't go with any of your friends."

"Not even Cressida?"

"Whatever," I said.

Squirrel asked Cressida and she said yes. He borrowed his brother's Camaro, even though he didn't have a license. The car barely had a backseat, but four of us managed to squeeze in. Cress was in shotgun, and Deep and I were in back next to Richie Cohen and Jane, who were lap-sitting.

Squirrel sort of knew how to drive. He only stalled at lights, or when it was his turn to hit the joint. Richie held my sister across the waist, and I knew she liked it even though she was terrified.

Jane still talks about that ride like it's the most dangerous thing she's ever done. "Fifteen with open containers and narcotics. We're lucky we didn't die." She sounds like an after-school special.

For Jane it was a one-timer: reckless youth, laughed over now. I won't say it's because Grandpa never touched her that she turned out normal and I didn't. That's what my therapist says, but she's wrong.

I think, mostly, the problem was my parents and their shitty DNA. Sometimes, people with absent parents are forced to grow up too fast. I was the opposite; I stayed a child. Jane grew up for me; that's what twins are for.

In that backseat we were reunited. Jane hit a joint for the first time, and Squirrel ran over a squirrel.

The dance was in the cafeteria, which had been made to look like the future. Everything was silver foil, and the nerds were dressed in expensive-looking *Star Trek* costumes. The DJ played cheesy techno, and Squirrel kissed Cress from the get-go, off in the corner, hands clutching her butt. Deep and I walked circles complaining about the music. Sis and Richie danced slow, arms extended and parallel.

At the center of the dance floor was Celia, alight in gold tights and Princess Leia double-buns. She danced the way she interacted with her friends—not *with*, but *about*—orbiting, distracted, rhythmically aligned to the offbeat, the drummer's spaces. The rat-a-tat-tat-ness came from inside her, as if her body's movements controlled the music and not the other way around.

I watched from a distance, standing still, forgetting the other people, and that I was no longer allowed to stare. She danced alone, no boys in sight. I watched her dip between people, spinning like a slo-mo top, pirouette perfect as a windup doll's. "Stop staring at her," Deep said.

There was a party after. We weren't supposed to know about it, but someone told someone and Squirrel had a car. Jose's parents were out of town.

There was a white felt pool table in the living room. Out back it was like every movie about high school. Girls swam in bras, splashing, giggling. Deep and I played our roles. We sat in the corner with a small plastic bong. Squirrel and Cress had gone upstairs. There were empty rooms upstairs: guest rooms, the maid's room. I wondered where Celia was. I hoped she wasn't upstairs. I imagined her upstairs.

Richie had walked Jane to the door of our house, and we'd made smooching sounds and laughed.

The party was boring because no one talked to Deep and me, and we acted like we didn't want anyone to talk to us. We stole graham crackers and set up shop in the treehouse, smoking cigarettes and taking slugs from the unboxed silver foil bag of red wine that Squirrel's brother had given us with the advice, "If you give her enough of this shit, she'll at least let you finger her."

Deep wasn't much of a talker. "Fuck this shit," he said, and I said, "Yeah, fuck this shit," and we continued saying things like that, or variations: I'd fuck the shit out of these bitches, if these bitches want to fuck with me I'll fuck them up, maybe that fuckin' bitch will want to lick my shit and then fuck that shit, fuckin' A, fuck double fuck.

The sun came up. Celia woke in a deck chair. She stood and stretched, unaware of being watched. She reached for a pack of cigarettes on the table and pulled one to her lip. She fumbled for a lighter, looked around, and saw me.

I reached into my pocket, held up my lighter. Celia nodded.

I walked toward her, dancing off-balance around the empty beers and sleeping bodies. Celia shivered and wrapped her arms around her chest. I lit her cigarette and lit one for myself.

We didn't say anything, just watched the sunlight move across the yard, illuminating the sleeping bodies as if they were casualties of war, sinking into the dew. I thought of my grandfather, of his body, its spots and abscesses, its whiteness.

Celia exhaled. The smoke was so visible in the wet air that it looked like a cartoon speech-bubble coming from her mouth. I wanted to fill it with words.

"Hi," I said.

"Are you okay?" she said in a timid voice, as if she didn't want to disrupt the morning's calm.

"I'm sorry," I said. "About . . ."

"I'm sorry," she said.

I knew that if there was ever a moment to kiss her, it was now. I also knew that now was not the moment to kiss her, and that there never would be one.

•   •   •

Grandpa died that summer. First he shat himself often, forgot I was Sam or that anyone was anyone, became incoherent, repeated phrases like "No one's waiting" and "This body is not this body."

DECEMBER BOYS
GOT IT BAD

Lawrence and I have lost our jobs. We walk the bridge toward Brooklyn, where it's cool to be poor. We don't call our mothers. It's warm for September, and we strip in the sunlight. Lawrence tosses his sport coat over the rail. The wind doesn't take it; no fluttering kitelike, symbolic and cinematic. It sinks into traffic, under tires, another piece of highway trash. I hesitate before tossing mine.

"Blow winds and crack your cheek!" Lawrence cries. "Rage! Blow! Spout 'til you have wet my codpiece! I give my garments of oppression to the open sea!"

A man standing near us says, "That nigga's crazy."

He's about five two, with a port-wine stain that covers most of his face and neck. Teeth misaligned and T-shirt too small—tight over ribs, holes under armpits.

"He saw Lear in the park," I say.

"That must make you the Fool," the man says, and laughs a mucus-loosening laugh.

Lawrence is shirtless now, showing off the tattoo he got one two a.m. in the East Village while half blacked out and impressing a girl. It's a Native American dream catcher, in rainbow colors, wrapped around his rib cage.

"Fellow proletarian," Lawrence addresses the man, "we are brothers, huddled on this bridge among the masses of the unemployed. We're America's castoffs. They said bring us your hungry, and they lied. They meant bring them to Brooklyn, let them suffer in slums. We're nature's toilets now."

"You live in a townhouse," I say, but Lawrence isn't listening.

Our new friend, however, is.

"What you call me, white boy? I ain't your brother, motherfucker. I ain't no proletarian"

"Do you wear Brooks Brothers?" I say, and hand the man my garment of oppression.

It's four sizes too big. In it, he's a child, someone's younger brother. He rolls up the cuffs and pretends there's a mirror.

"Not typically my style," the man says.

"You can get it tailored," I say, and push Lawrence forward.

We're accosted by a roaming documentarian. He waves a smartphone in our faces, narrates: "Here we have the junior investment banker, Latin name *Douchebagius ecco homophobe*. An endangered species and a rare sight en route to the outer boroughs."

Lawrence is in love with the camera. He's in love with himself in this moment. He's waving a middle finger and glugging from the pint of bourbon we bought back in Manhattan after being pink-slipped. He hands me the bottle. I sip and then offer it to our homeless friend, who declines.

"Been straight since summer of '69," he says. "I got weepy at the moon landing. It's been clean living ever since."

"Tell the world," Lawrence tells the camera phone. "I'm more sinned against than sinner! Wall Street has taken our salaries, but it will never take our souls!"

The first bar on the other side has a hundred beers on tap and overpriced wings dripping with watery hot sauce.

"The blood of the factory-farmed chicken," Lawrence says, licks his finger.

He saw some documentary. He's wearing my button-down, bar appropriate. I'm down to a T-shirt. My arms aren't muscled like Lawrence's. They're bone-thin, sun-sheltered, ghostly white.

"Eat up," Lawrence says. "Gather strength for the bacchanal. And would it kill you to join a gym?"

"Never had the time," I say, and finally feel the truth of my new freedom: the onslaught of open hours, days unfolding like an origami fortune-teller.

I've always been a workaholic, the product of a siblingless childhood. So many nights spent in midwestern solitude, TV busted and the world half a dream with its sensory feints: the cricket-chirp quiet and grease-burger air, sun over cornfields goldening everything.

But math felt solid, composed of proven truths. I pored over equations, spreadsheet cells, PowerPoint presentations; Xs, Ys, and dollar signs; worked my way through business school and onto Wall Street. I tried to move figures so that everyone would benefit—clients, Lehman, plus the public—as the market shifted and swerved. Now our work's been exposed as faulty, a mess of fragile systems, theoretically unsound. I feel implicated, even if the orders came from on high.

Tonight's the result: postponing despair by pounding Jäger bombs and listening to Lawrence rant.

"Fräulein!" Lawrence calls to the waitress.

"Don't be an asshole," I say.

"Get over the six million already," Lawrence says. "Germany is a forward-thinking country. Fräulein!"

He's standing, waving.

The waitress saunters over, used to types like us. She too is costumed, a facsimile Bavarian wench. Her breasts are pressed between suspenders, barely contained. They hang over her corset like cartoon eye bags.

"My name's Kim, I'm gay and taken, and the bathroom's to the left," she says, anticipating all of Lawrence's requests.

Kim flashes a ringed finger. It shines blingy in the bar light.

"Conflict diamonds," says Lawrence. "How many have been killed in Sierra Leone so you can rub your queer lifestyle in our faces?"

"It's cubic zirconium," Kim says.

"Chill," I say to Lawrence, and touch his arm.

Kim walks away smiling, impenetrable. I imagine

Kim and her fiancée drinking OJ in a breakfast nook, laughing over egg whites, reading aloud from the Sunday paper.

"I should have gone into commodities," I say. "The American dream is orange juice."

"This is a shit restaurant," Lawrence says. "The Internet lied to me. There were no hot wings in Hitler's time. Am I the last of the true believers?"

Still, we tip well.

"We're going to meet some artsy chicks," Lawrence says. "Commune with them in class solidarity. We can namedrop that kid from high school who went to Wesleyan and plays in that band now."

"Alec Emmer," I say. "It's not a band. It's a collective."

"He used to be a faggot," Lawrence says. "Now he gets more pussy than anyone. There's a lesson there."

The lesson involves buying tighter pants than we normally wear.

"Can I help you?" the salesgirl asks.

She's thin and curveless; confident, Parisian-striped, no older than nineteen. Silver eyeliner's painted in raccoon streaks that triangulate toward her ears.

"Outfit us," Lawrence intones. "Armor us in a garb fit for dance halls and bohemian debutantes."

He adds, "Make us look gay, but not too gay."

"I can work with that," the salesgirl says.

The fitting-room mirror makes me look ugly: top-heavy, visibly acne-scarred. Or maybe I was already ugly.

Lawrence grins, flexes. He helps me button the too-tight pants, adjusts my bulge. It tingles. I have an urge to hug his body to my body, not in a sexual way, but out of what feels like purer longing; I want skin on my skin, hot breath up my nostrils, fingers easing the knots in my neck while Lawrence hums Easter hymns and I weep into his bosom.

"Lawrence," I say, and squeeze his arm. His bicep bubbles under my thumb.

Lawrence ignores whatever it is I'm doing.

"You want it to be horizontal in these pants," he says. "And semistiff. It's a visual mating call. Tuck it up there. Show some shaft."

When the salesgirl sees our new outfits she says, "Oh, no, that doesn't work at all."

She points, shakes her head. "Let me see if we have that in a size up," she says.

"I knew you'd say that," Lawrence says. "I'm psychic. I bet I can guess the first three digits of your phone number."

"And if you do?"

"You find a friend and meet us at that place on the corner with the blue awning when you get off work."

"That's not for four hours," she says.

"Seven one eight," Lawrence snaps.

"Area code doesn't count," she says, but Lawrence is already gloating.

He calls her Raccoon Eyes. Does a leprechaun dance, arms flailing, knees akimbo. Sings the first verse of "Rocky Raccoon."

"You fucker," the salesgirl says in the way of someone charmed despite herself.

•   •   •

We go to the bar with the blue awning. Sit in a corner booth and pretend the girls are coming. Lawrence texts his dealer. I put my head on the table, feel the oil against my forehead. Wish I'd taken more comp-sci classes in college. Imagine what my office would be like if I worked at Google: pastel walls, bay view, maybe one of those yoga-ball chairs.

"Goddamnit, Alejandro, answer your phone," says Lawrence. "The revolution can't be fueled by blood and beer alone."

Two booths over, our former waitress cozies up to the woman who must be her girlfriend. The girlfriend is tattooed, tiny, terribly pretty, with a half-shaved head that flatters her perfect facial symmetry. Kim's still in her work costume. They hold hands under the table, lean into each other, nuzzle necks and ears. If this were a movie, I'd buy them a round, wave from a bar stool, whisper, "Men might be scum, but some of us believe in love."

"Pick up your goddamn phone," Lawrence says.

It's five hours later. We're on Lawrence's roof, overlooking the promenade. Bridge lit up, and Manhattan just beyond, so close it seems fake, a full-scale model. One of those romantic New York tableaux that only makes you feel alone, partnerless. The stars are out. Lawrence yells, "The stars are out, motherfucker!"

He raises his arms like a football ref signaling touchdown.

His girl laughs. She thinks we're losers in a cute way. She says, "You guys are such losers."

The cute part's implied.

My girl stares at the water, grimaces, exhales, boot-crushes her cigarette, gives me a look like "*What?*"

I don't know how or why or when we decided which girl was whose, but Lawrence got the flirtier end of that bargain—Rocky Raccoon.

She's on his lap, leaning to tap into the ashtray, showing off tiny, braless breasts in her T-shirt's low V. She's dressed the same as before, but she's lipsticked now, a blood shade of red. Big lips stain her cigarette, dwarf it. Lawrence wraps an arm all the way around her waist.

"So you guys know the band Lazy Rat?" he says.

"Lazer Rat," I correct.

"The collective?" Rocky asks.

"Same thing," Lawrence says. "Anyway, Alec Emmer from Lazer Cat's gonna come by in a bit. He's an old friend of mine."

I give him a look.

Lawrence adds, "Of ours," indicating me with a weak nod.

A memory returns: Lawrence spray-painting "Retardo" on Alec Emmer's car.

"I met Alec Emmer once," my girl says. It's the first thing she's said in an hour. "I gave him a blow job after a show at Brooklyn Bowl. He had the loveliest dick I've ever seen. Just perfectly circumcised."

"Where was I that night?" Rocky asks.

"With your ex," my girl says. "Remember him?"

"Don't remind me," Rocky says, smiles, pats Lawrence's head.

"Are some dicks *im*perfectly circumcised?" I ask. I'm actually curious.

"Yeah," Rocky says. "Uncircumcised ones."

"Too bad Emmer's a homo," Lawrence says, annoyed. "Or you all could have married him."

He pulls Rocky closer, claiming her.

"Let's go inside," Lawrence says.

The girls have never seen a banker's place. Didn't know bankers even *lived* in Brooklyn. Rocky has a tiny anarchist's *A* tattooed on the back of one elbow. Lawrence's home is alien, exotic, erotically out of line with her professed values. It has leather furniture, colored lightbulbs in the lamps.

Rocky inspects every inch. Like an amateur anthropologist. Runs a finger along the edge of the flat screen, blows dust from her finger. Opens cabinets, caresses cookware, cuddles the couch pillows.

Lawrence sings, *"Rocky Raccoon, came into my room, and proceeded to feel up my trinkets."*

He shows off his collections: samurai swords, gator-gutting knives, fish-gutting knives, bear-gutting knives, machetes, Nazi armbands, a Civil War musket, fraternity paddles used for beating freshman ass in a strictly heterosexual manner.

My girl's unimpressed. She sits silent, condescending, opening and closing her cell phone, unaware that she's my girl.

Her name's Nina. She's a freshman at Pratt. They both are. Studio art majors. Never heard of Rothko. Lawrence shows them a first-edition monograph, purchased for big chowder at the rare books place on Eighth Avenue.

"I don't go for that mainstream stuff," says Rocky. "It's like, painting is so old-fashioned. All those giant canvases covered in semen. We get it already, you know?"

Lawrence—whom I once saw weep loudly in MoMA at a giant red dreamscape—raises his frat paddle at Rocky in a gesture of half-kidding disapproval.

"Ew, you were in a frat," Nina accuses. "What a cliché."

"A communist brotherhood," Lawrence replies, and unhooks the full-length mirror from the wall, balances it atop the coffee table, lays out fat lines of what I know, from past experience, to be fairly weak cocaine.

Now Nina's interested. She takes a picture of the coke on her phone. Says she'll use it for an upcoming mixed-media project that explores the relationship between commerce and chauvinism. Kneels over the mirror, huffs her rail in three phlegmy snorts, stands, wipes her nose, licks her fingers, slicks her bangs back.

It's the first time all night that I've seen Nina's face. She has high, rouged cheekbones and hardly any nose at all. Maybe the product of Waspy stock—a Greenwich escapee, guiltily funded, brow-pierced and playing at gutter punk. Her green eyes shine under Lawrence's mood lights. She wears spandex and a loose V-neck that barely covers her butt. The phrase "Kill Me I Love Love" is stenciled on the shirt in Magic Marker. It looks like a nightgown. Her hands are Sharpied in fading Xs.

"What the fuck are you looking at?" Nina says.

Lawrence puts on music, embarrassing music, club trance from his raver phase in high school.

"Are you kidding?" Nina says, but Lawrence isn't listening. He's in private concert with himself: head bopping, legs kicking as he makes inadvisable spins and gyrations.

"The beat is my only friend!" Lawrence yells. "The beat is alive in Brooklyn! It's my heartbeat, in sync with the nation. America, I've given you everything, now give me music!"

Rocky's inspired. She slinks up to Lawrence, circles him, twiddles fingers, bites bottom lip, bends low, slithers. Lawrence pretends he doesn't notice. Just shakes his head to the beat and yells, "Brooklyn," again.

Rocky grabs his butt cheeks, presses groin against groin.

"Cigarette?" I say to Nina.

We climb the fire escape to the roof. I go first, then offer my hand from the top of the ladder. Nina ignores my offer. She pulls herself up with some difficulty.

I sit with legs over the edge. They dangle semidangerously, swaying like loose chimes. Brooklyn's below, a concrete cityscape littered with construction sites. Over in Fort Greene the new buildings are rising, high condominiums that ugly our skyline. I could fall right now, drop three stories from this townhouse roof. It would take only a moment—no real hang time. But in that moment the air would push against me like a set of strong hands.

"I'm sorry I'm no fun," Nina says.

She sits behind me, cross-legged, safe from the ledge and the reach of my arms. I turn to face her. Her knees buckle out in bony contortion, stretch the fabric of her spandex.

"I'm not really such a bitch," she says.

"You don't seem like a bitch," I say, and it's true. She just seems young, appropriately guarded, stuck on Rocky's sleazy date as the air turns cool and the drugs don't work like they're supposed to.

Nina shivers. I hand her my new sweatshirt.

"Thanks," she says, and pulls the strings so the hood closes over her eyes.

I toss a bottle. It breaks in the street below. I stand, pace in circles, pinch my forehead, reseat myself. Nina opens a beer but doesn't sip.

"That coke is weak as fuck," she says.

"Yeah," I say. "That's why he buys so much of it. Eventually it'll get you high."

"If we're ever allowed back inside," she says, and cracks a smile of annoyed camaraderie.

I'm used to the situation: Lawrence boning with abandon; me outside, forcing banter. Maybe Nina's used to it too.

Without prompt I picture Alec Emmer hovering above her, dick dripping semen on her unblemished face. It's a vulgar image, received from pornography, the international symbol of dénouement.

"Did you really hook up with Alec Emmer?"

"Nah. I was just fucking with you guys. I've never even heard of him."

"Serves Lawrence right," I say, and inch toward Nina.

I'm close enough to put a hand on the small of her back. This is the last thing I should do. She's not even twenty. Coke sex is always sad. I probably couldn't get it up.

"It's my fault," I say, unsure what exactly I'm referring to.

"What's your fault?" she says.

"Everything," I say.

I want her to say no, no it's not, it's not your fault, baby, nothing is your fault.

We make eye contact. Or maybe I force eye contact. Maybe my hand moves just a tiny bit toward her. Maybe there's a ripple in the front of my jeans, an odor of longing coming off me, a lip lick, some giveaway tic, evidence that I'm about to lean in.

Nina scoots in the other direction.

I start to say something about life, the way things change and the past gets pushed aside, yet still, yet still, we're haunted. And we fight through the sludge, and we fail, keep failing, just keep fucking failing.

But I sound like an asshole.

Nina stares at the bridge. Cars squeal and honk. She says, "Speak for yourself."

Lawrence and Rocky emerge from the fire escape. They're in matching, monogrammed bathrobes. An old Christmas gift from Lawrence's ex, Inez, the only girl who ever got his jokes.

Rocky's face is red, colored from exertion. She smiles, sucks a cigarette, squeezes Lawrence's hand.

"What have *you* two been up to?" she asks conspiratorially, as if we're the ones who've been sexing.

Nina and I say nothing.

"What happens on the roof stays on the roof," Lawrence says. No one laughs.

The sky's gone cloudy, stars under cover. We're heading toward sunrise, but the night hasn't lightened; no pinks yet or earthy coppers. I'm cold in my T-shirt. A couple of wet drops touch my neck.

Rocky leaves Lawrence, hooks elbows with Nina, ushers her across the roof for closed cabal. Lawrence walks to where I'm standing. He puts his hands on my shoulders like he's asking to slow dance. He says, "Let your horrible pleasure fall."

SOME NIGHTS WE TASE EACH OTHER

In college I read Karl Marx and snorted cocaine. The Marx I didn't much understand. The cocaine contextualized.

I lived with four other guys. We weren't a classless household. Some were subsidized: parentally, governmentally. Others worked campus jobs. This one roommate—Spine, we called him, because he didn't have one—was from that town in Connecticut where the mansions come pre-equipped with bowling alleys.

Spine was our procurer, doled to the rest as he saw fit. He took payment in the form of term papers. I was caught in an *ouroboros* of needing drugs to complete Spine's papers, and writing papers to pay for drugs. Spine was getting Cs across the board but didn't care. He had a gig lined up after grad, at a cushy desk selling commercial real estate for some blueblood uncle.

One night I'm battling a twenty-pager on labor theory when I hear this noise downstairs—breaking glass. It's about two a.m.

Spine bursts into the hall holding a baseball bat. He's wearing boxers and a bathrobe. Through his open door I can see two girls tangled, loose limbs dangling. One girl has toenails painted in rainbow. The other has an ankle tattoo of an ankh. Neither girl is Spine's girlfriend. It's another injustice, though I'm not sure for whom. As far as I could tell, Marx wanted women to be passed around, shared among workers.

"The fuck was that?" Spine says, tightens his grip on the bat. The others emerge. Mike F. brandishes the police Taser he bought on eBay. Some nights we Tase each other. Donny fans his butterfly knife. Mike C. cracks his knuckles. More noise from the living room, a loud scurrying.

"Shit on a brick," Spine says.

Downstairs, there's a guy. A black guy, I should say, because it makes a difference. The difference is we want black people to like us. None of us had black friends growing up. In college, the black kids stay separate, have their own a cappella group.

The black guy in our living room looks only marginally homeless. He smells of wet ink and burnt plastic. Has holes in his Nikes, holes in his sweater. His lips are dry and tinted white.

We circle. The intruder brushes glass from his body like he's unaware we're watching, wielding weapons. He scratches his arms, mumbles under his breath.

"Hey, guy," Mike C. says.

And suddenly the intruder's snapped out of his daze, borne into motion. He grabs one of Spine's guitars—they're mounted on the wall—holds it two-handed from the neck like he's about to hit a backhand. But the guitar is heavy; the intruder's arms buckle under the Gibson's weight. Instead of swinging at us, or dropping the ax and hustling back out through the window, the intruder sits on the glassy floor and begins to play.

The guitar is Spine's pride and joy—a semihollow ES-335 with cherry finish—his favorite of the five guitars he owns. I've seen him polish the thing for over an hour.

The intruder strums the open strings, plucks a C chord, fingers a dainty little lead. Then he starts crying.

"Fuckin' A," Mike F. says.

We're still surrounding the guy. I don't have a weapon, but I notice I'm holding Spine's laptop like I might smash skull. Mike F. flicks the Taser on and off, pockets it. Mike C. unballs his fists. Donny's knife is back in chrysalis. I put the laptop on the coffee table. Spine's still gripping the bat. The intruder's still crying. The girls, wearing Spine's T-shirts, watch from the staircase. They grip each other's arms. One shirt says "Legend" in gold lamé.

I fill a glass of water. The intruder wipes his tears. He sniffs the water.

"Smell all right?" Donny says.

The intruder nods, takes a small sip, then a bigger one. He clears his throat, prepped to make a proclamation.

"Cigarette," the intruder says. The voice is thin and weak, like an un-amped guitar—no sustain.

Spine fishes a cig from his bathrobe pocket. He lights

it himself, hands it off to the intruder. For a second their fingers touch.

The intruder takes a deep drag, exhales through his nose. The rest of us stand staring. The intruder eyes our apartment. The floor is covered in trash and hardened socks. On the ceiling hangs a tie-dye banner with Bob Marley's face silkscreened in the middle.

Outside it's raining. The wind carries rain in through the broken window. It's the end of April, and it gets cold at night. The intruder is shivering. He takes another long drag, sticks the cig between guitar strings.

Spine nervously watches, bracing for ash marks on the neck of his ax. I imagine he's thinking of the story down the line, the way he'll tell it at a party one day—the guy who broke in and played the blues, scarred the cherry Gibson with a cigarette tattoo, imbued it with a hint of hard living.

"How about a beer?" the intruder asks. His voice sounds louder now, more sure.

Donny grabs two from the fridge, tosses one over, pops the other for himself.

The intruder takes a slug. He licks his lips and says, "Ah."

I sit on the La-Z-Boy. Spine, Donny, and Mike F. are on the couch. No one's picking up the broken glass. We don't have a dustpan. The girls have moved into the doorway, and the intruder has noticed.

"Hello there," he says, and smiles for the first time. He's missing half a front tooth. The girls look like kids at a grown-up party, pulled from sleep by parents for the party guests' amusement.

Spine points a finger at the intruder. "Watch it," he says.

For a second we tense. Spine looks at the bat. Then he laughs, hard. He actually slaps his knee.

Mike C. packs a bowl, sparks it. Spine picks up another guitar, this one an acoustic. He hammers out twelve-bar in E, playing ninths to show off, sliding up and down the neck.

The intruder tries to keep up. He's not as good as Spine, but knows the pentatonic scale, a couple riffs.

Spine grins like an idiot, says, "Play it, babe."

We take hits off the bowl. I look at the girls' legs, wonder how their thighs got so tan. I try to see if they're wearing underwear. The girls wrap themselves in a wool blanket stitched with the Coca-Cola logo.

Mike F.'s got his bass now, joined in on the jam. Donny slaps at an African hand drum. One girl—Ankle—pulls a bag from Spine's pocket, lays out lines on the table. The intruder perks up, puts down the guitar.

"You first," Spine says. He hands the intruder a rolled up hundred. The intruder looks skeptical. He snorts and hands the hundred back to Spine, making a show of his non-stealing.

Next thing I know he's standing, singing. Spine, Mike F., and Donny accompany.

"I broke into a house." Ba-wah, ba-wah.

"Wasn't soft as a mouse." Ba-wah, ba-wah.

"Thought these white boys would kill me." Ba-wah, ba-wah.

"Gonna drill me and beat me."

"Gonna grill me and eat me."

We're all laughing, even the girls. Spine has that Connecticut smile going, the kind that whispers, "I've won at life!" His blue eyes actually sparkle. The girls swoon. The intruder continues.

"But they give me a smoke." Ba-wah, ba-wah.

"And they give me a toke." Ba-wah, ba-wah.

"And they give me some coke." Ba-wah, ba-wah.

At this, the intruder leans over and huffs another rail. Comes back in on the next bar, still in time.

"Now there's just one more thing." Ba-wah, ba-wah.

"That my new friends can bring." Ba-wah, ba-wah.

"Make me scream cry and beg."

"Wait for it," Spine says.

"For a touch on those legs!"

The intruder winks at the girls, sticks out his tongue.

"Ew," says Ankle, furrowing her upturned, tiny nose. Toes appears not to have heard.

"Hey now," Spine says.

It occurs to me that everyone is very high. The intruder takes another cigarette from the pack out on the table.

"You got a name?" Spine says.

"Jess," the intruder says.

"A girl's name," Spine says.

"That's right," Jess says.

"Well, Jess," says Spine, "we can't let you steal any of our shit."

"Ba-wah, Ba-wah," Jess says.

The rain's coming harder now. Jess looks out the window. I see the rest of his night flash before him, the way it will go when we kick him out and he comes down. The rain won't let up until morning.

"There's a couch on the covered porch, though," Spine says. "If you want to crash."

• • •

Around this time, I was coming to terms with my lot in life. May came on, clothes came off—first sweaters, then socks and stockings—barefoot coeds sunning in the quad, books splayed across burnt stomachs.

I was onto Trotsky now, dreaming of Mexico. I sat in my room while the others partied downstairs with Jess; I listened to mariachi, sniffed imagined bougain-villea, ate takeout enchiladas. When I closed my eyes I saw Leon in that freight train, groggy head resting on a rice bag, rolling through Tampico at dusk. I saw Frida Kahlo slow-riding him, eyebrows arched, twisting the corners of his mustache with her fingers. Some nights I could feel the sweep of Stalin's ice pick through the center of my brain.

A knock on the door.

"Entrez-vous," I say.

There stands Isabelle—Spine's actual girlfriend— slouched like a sunflower too heavy for its stem. She wears a thin linen dress belted high above her navel. My room is dim, lamp-lit, and in the shadowy doorway she looks almost like a silhouette, features blurred, but the shape of her apparent: heavy breasts, the crescent curve of calves.

I'm on the futon mattress, back propped against the wall. My immediate instinct is to take cover under blan-kets, hide myself in the face of Isabelle's beauty.

Isabelle has told me that I'm like a brother to her, her best friend. These are awful words, the plight of the sensi-tive man. I've been battling them for years. Isabelle picks a book up off my desk, flicks the pages, puts it down. She takes a cigarette from my pack but doesn't light it. She puts the unlit cig behind her ear.

"New roommate seems interesting," she says. Her eyes flitter across my bookshelf, scanning for fresh purchases. She doesn't look at me. Her eyes are green.

"That's the word for him," I say. "Interesting. The situation is, well, I don't know exactly."

"Well, Robert is certainly infatuated," she says, using Spine's given name.

"That's Spine for you," I say.

"Spine, Spine, Spine," she says, and lies down on the futon, inches from me, head on the pillow. Isabelle smells like shampoo and the faintest trace of sweat. We've reclined like this a hundred times, but still my heartbeat quickens.

I could slip beneath the linen, hold my palm against her panties, feel the heat coming off her.

Sometimes I think she wouldn't stop me. I've never tried. Spine finds my friendship with Isabelle amusing and pathetic.

"So he broke in," she says, "and you let him move in with you." She's trying to sound exasperated but can't hide that she's impressed.

"Spine let him," I say. "And he hasn't moved in. He's just crashing for a while."

"Shit on a brick," Isabelle says, imitating Spine's nasal whine.

I snatch the cigarette from behind her ear, walk to the window, lean against the sill, and smoke. Isabelle crawls under the duvet, oblivious. If I told Isabelle about Ankle and Toes, it would only make things worse. She would tell me to fuck off. She might hit me. She would wait to cry until she was alone. She would let herself believe whatever lies Spine would spin to fix the situation.

Telling her I love her wouldn't help the matter either.

"You figure out your summer plan?" she says.

"Still working at the bookstore," I say.

"What about Paris?" she says. "Me, you, and Robert, smoking in cafés? I thought that was on?"

I see myself alone at a bar, fumbling with my French, waiting for them to finish fucking so I can reenter the hotel room.

"Too expensive," I say.

"Suit yourself," she says. "It's too bad, though—so many beautiful women in Paris. I figured we could find you one."

Later on, I can hear them. Spine grunts from the gut. Isabelle sounds like a bird, no, not a bird, more like a bell—clean tone, natural vibrato. I imagine her mouth open wide, the tremor of her tonsils, the rush of air coming out.

Donny worked at Campus Convenience. Twice a week during his afternoon shift, Donny's boss's and his co-worker's lunch breaks coincided, leaving Donny alone in the store for twenty minutes. When the coast was clear, Donny would call us on the house phone and scream, "Biotch!" into the answering machine. We'd grab back-packs and go, cleaning out the aisles, stocking up on freezer supplies.

Spine insists that Jess come along.

"I don't know, man," Jess says. "Sounds off to me." Jess bites his bitten nails, looks sideways at Spine.

"Not off," Spine says. "Easy."

Spine pulls on one of those full-face ski masks with holes cut out for eyes.

"Trust me, baby," Spine says.

"Take that fucking mask off," I say. "This isn't a movie."

"Seems off," Jess says, and shakes his head. "Something's not right."

We run through the aisles, adrenalized. I feel sexy and alive. We steal Slim Jims, Ritz crackers, gummy worms. Jess is in and out in a matter of seconds with only a Snickers bar to show for it.

"I ain't playin'," he says, when we're back home.

That night we feast. Spine buys one of those three-foot sausages from Stop and Shop, and we cut it in pieces to top our stolen frozen pizzas. We mix vodka with Mountain Dew, smoke joints and cigarillos.

Jess minimally partakes. I've never seen him eat. I get the sense that he's waiting, watching and waiting for Spine to lay out the lines, conspiratorially hand Jess a rolled up hundred, whisper, "Play it, babe."

It's getting toward dawn. We're high as skyscrapers, looking over the mountainous heaps of our living room city, scraping smatterings of powder, the dregs of Spine's stash. Ankle and Toes are twitchy, moody. They've stopped massaging Spine's neck and shoulders. They lie head to foot on the nasty floor, staring up at Bob Marley, listening to Spine play some slow fingerpick. Jess sways, smiles. Spine scratches his chin.

What Spine wants is for Jess to lead the way, searching the city streets for one last hit.

"I don't know, man," Jess says. "This ain't the hour."

"Buddy," Spine says. He's got a hand on Jess's shoulder, and he speaks in a calm, low voice like he's a boxing coach, coaxing his fighter in for one last round. "Now or never, dawg," Spine says.

We walk outside. The sun lingers on the horizon, threatening to burst the graying black. The streets and lawns smell like dew. Jess leads us. We follow, trancelike, weaving over Longfellow Bridge as the skyline approaches. We've been walking for an hour. I'm sweating, half asleep, or maybe I'm sleepwalking and the morning is a surreal dream: this sleeping city, our holey leader, Spine, humming the blues.

Jess leads us through the Chinatown gates into the old Combat Zone. I remember hearing stories about this place: the night-beat hookers asleep on benches, fishnet legs fetally curled; cops hitting the homeless with nightsticks; human corpses laid out with the morning trash.

Things are different these days. The city is quiet. The streets are empty. It smells of fish. Jess tells us to give him all our money.

For a second we hesitate, look up at the building, back at Jess. His hands are in his pockets.

Spine takes out his wallet, peels off a fresh fifty. The rest of us give Jess tens and twenties. Jess crumples the money in his palm. Whatever we're getting, we're overpaying. Jess says to wait outside.

We light cigarettes almost in unison, blow smoke at the remaining stars as they shine weakly against the gray and coming blue. We check our watches.

Jess reappears ten minutes later, grinning. We follow him to the harbor, watch the ocean lap its waves. Jess pulls a bag from his pocket. It looks like pebbles.

Walking back to Cambridge, as the sun warms my body, I feel like part of the people's cavalry, its vestigial remains.

The next day Donny calls us in for another round of theft. Jess doesn't come along. Says he's too tired, needs some shuteye. He says *shuteye* like it's a word he's only just learned.

When we get back to the house everything is gone: instruments, plasma TV, stereo equipment, all our laptops.

"Shit on a brick," Spine says. "Shit on a goddamn, motherfucking brick."

Jess must have had help, known a guy with a van. Our furniture's gone too—Spine's king bed, even the corduroy couch with all the rips and burns.

At first, it's hard to believe. I stare at the empty living room as if the stuff is still there but I'm just not seeing it, not looking hard enough.

A smile slowly opens on Spine's face. His lips snake toward his ears. Spine starts to laugh.

"He deserved it," Spine says. "He deserved it all."

When Isabelle knocks on my door that night I don't say a word. I'm under covers with the lights off, listening to our next-door neighbor play piano. I've been having trouble sleeping. The neighbor repeats the opening bars of some famous overture, a piece I recognize from movies but could never name.

Isabelle enters anyway, climbs into bed, lays her head against my chest. I lie perfectly still and try to slow my breathing. Isabelle adjusts herself, gets comfortable. She lays a leg over my legs.

"Spine passed out on the carpet," she says. "Took too much Klonopin."

"It's been a stressful day," I say.

"He thinks the whole thing is hilaaaaarious," she says, elongating her vowels in imitation of Spine. "Now he gets to go on a shopping spree. What an ass."

The hair on my arm stands from the static friction. The neighbor keeps screwing up on the exact same note and starting over.

"Why?" I say.

"Why what?"

"Why Spine?" I say. I run my fingers gently over her arm, just the tips. There is a long pause. Isabelle inhales like she's about to say something, then stops herself. She fidgets a little and I stop stroking her arm.

"Don't you see?" I say.

"See what?" Isabelle says.

I take a strand of her hair between my fingers. Isabelle says nothing. I only have to turn a tiny bit. I give the softest kiss I can, hardly a kiss at all, just closed lips brushing her ear.

"Don't," Isabelle says.

I roll on top of her, pin her arms to the mattress.

"Stop," she says.

I'm not the kind of guy who acts like no means yes even when it does. I try to wear this weakness as a badge of honor. I roll off Isabelle, sit up.

"I can't do this anymore," I say.

"Do what?" Isabelle says.

"I'm done," I say.

"Just come back and cuddle me," she says, and yawns. It's the yawn that gets me.

"No," I say. Isabelle pulls my arm.

"You're being dramatic," she says. "Come on."

"I'm done," I say.

"Fine," Isabelle says. She pulls herself up. I listen for her footsteps, let myself sink into the mattress. It feels like I could just keep sinking, falling through the floorboards, burrowing until I'm beneath the house itself, a mole to the earth's soft middle.

WE CLOSE OUR EYES

In the year following her hysterectomy, my mother befriended a priest. Before that, religion hadn't figured much into our family. We were secular Jews who didn't believe in God, went to temple once a year on Yom Kippur, and dabbled occasionally in Eastern thought. We'd all read *The Tao of Pooh*, but none of us got more than five pages into *The Te of Piglet*.

My own relationship with God existed solely through the prism of LSD, which I took whenever possible, ideally in star-soaked fields amid fresh-cut grass, but more likely in a basement with wall-to-wall carpeting and, possibly, a strobe light. I was sixteen and having a very difficult time getting laid.

I blamed this on numerous factors: that I went to a school where no one "got me"; that puberty hit me late, leaving me with a wispy attempt at sideburns and a voice

like a tone-deaf parakeet; that my doctor wouldn't pre-
scribe anything stronger than mouthwash for my halito-
sis. The main difficulty was probably the fact that I was
stoned all the time, but I saw it as more of a coping mech-
anism than cause. When I was stoned I was still horny, I
just didn't feel so angry about it. And when I was tripping,
my penis shriveled to half its size, and I might have forgot
it was there if I didn't so enjoy watching the trails of light
dance around my stream of urine as I pissed in the dirt or
in a pile of snow.

I also spent plenty of time masturbating. I left my seed
everywhere: on towels, shower curtains, pillow cases,
pieces of notebook paper, the pages of my mother's pho-
tography books (Man Ray was an early favorite), women's
fashion magazines, the mouse pad of our computer. I liked
to return days later, find the dried crusty jizz, crumble it
in my fingers. I imagined each wad as an unborn child.
Sometimes I would name them: William, Kathleen, Ru-
fus, Ezekiel. I didn't like having a priest around the house.

Not that I had a say in the matter. We were careful
around my mother since she'd had surgery. No one said,
"Since she'd had cancer," but that's what we meant. You
weren't supposed to say cancer or cervix, just surgery. She
picked up smoking for the first time since my sister was
born, and everyone kept quiet about it. "Your mother's
under a lot of stress," my father said.

Me too. I was failing three out of five classes, and
my sister was on the verge of becoming school slut. She
thought our father was having an affair.

"How do you know?" I asked her. We were on the way
to school in my car, which was actually my mother's old

Toyota, given to me when she was sick because she wasn't doing much driving.

"Mom was crying the other night."

"Mom's always crying."

"This was different. She just kept crying and crying."

"She's under a lot of stress."

"Dad left her there. He didn't come back until like one in the morning."

"I'm sure it's nothing. And you better not be putting out for Matt Poncett either."

"It's none of your business."

"Everyone will say you have genital warts."

"Matt's sweet."

"He's not sweet."

In sixth grade Matt had bitten the tail off the class hamster.

"Believe me," I said, "He's not sweet."

"And he doesn't have genital warts. That's just a rumor. I've seen his dick, and it's, like, totally normal."

"I don't want to hear about it."

We were almost at school.

"It's the most normal dick I've ever seen."

"How many dicks have you seen to compare it to?"

"Seven."

"You've seen seven dicks?"

"Well, only five not counting you and Dad."

"When have you seen my dick?"

"When we were little and we used to take baths together."

"That's not an accurate representation. It's grown a lot since then."

"I'm sure it has."

"I don't want you to think . . ."

"So six, then," she said. "Six regular size and one child size."

"It was only child size because I was a child at the time!"

"Whatever," she said.

I pulled into the junior lot. Almost hit Sally Danzig, I was so distracted. The sun was aimed at me like a dentist's lamp. I could barely make out Sally giving me the finger and mouthing the word *loser*.

Later that day, or maybe it was a different day—that whole spring blends together, bathed in Dijon yellow light like a three-hour Spanish film where the plot is hard to follow, but you get the gist of it, understand in the actress's vacant gaze that she'll never be the same again—I met Father Larry for the first time. I'd been at Mike's doing whippits in the shed, or in Weinberg's basement ripping the four-footer. When I pulled into the driveway, my mom was sitting on the front step with a man I'd never seen.

He wore the priest outfit. I'd always wondered if it was a black shirt over a white shirt, or a white patch on the neck of a black shirt.

Straight off, I pegged him as a lush and an Irishman—the kind of Boston McDrunk priest you see in movies molesting little boys. They passed a cigarette and sipped from Styrofoam Dunkin' cups.

The tulips in the front garden had come up, yellow and white. Every morning my father had been out there planting, watering. Sometimes I'd watch through my bedroom window. From my vantage it looked as if he were digging through the earth like a blind dog.

"This is Father Lawrence," my mother said.

"Call me Larry."

"Zach," I said.

"Zachariah," he said.

"Just Zach," I said.

"Where have you been?" my mother said.

"At Molly's."

Molly was my imaginary girlfriend. I used her to quell suspicion about my drug use. If I'd said I was at Weinberg's, mom would know I'd been taking b-rips. She would call them b-rips too, because she'd overheard me say it.

"When are we going to meet this Molly?" my mother said.

"A good Irish name," Father Larry said.

It was two shirts, I was pretty sure.

"Hello?" my mother said, waving her hand in front of my face.

"You'll meet her."

"You could at least show us a picture."

"What does she look like?" Father Larry said. "A pretty one, I bet."

"She has tits like cantaloupes," I said.

It was the first thing that came to mind. And it wasn't even true!—I'd always imagined my imaginary girlfriend to be waifish.

"Zachary!" my mother said.

"Excuse me, Father," I said. "I meant eyes like cantaloupes, not tits. Her eyes are orange like cantaloupes."

"That doesn't even make sense," my mother said. "What is she, a cat?"

The priest laughed. "Young love," he said.

"Have you been sucking down jayskis?" my mother said.

"What?"

"Are you smoking ill nugs of kindbud?"

"You sound ridiculous," I said. "I have to go in and do homework."

"It's been a pleasure, Zach," Father Larry said.

I didn't do homework. Instead, I lay on my waterbed—another parental hand-me-down because it had been making my mother nauseous during chemo—and pretended I was floating. I wondered how many times my parents had had sex in this very bed, how many positions they'd used.

That night at dinner I said, "What's the deal with you and that priest?"

Mom blushed and said, "He's a poet, you know. He writes these wonderful poems about the earth and seasons. Very Zen. Sort of Zen-Catholic. You guys would like him."

"How did you meet him?" Ramona said.

"He works in the hospital. He goes around and talks to sick people."

"Shouldn't they have given you a rabbi for that?" I said.

"I don't know. He just showed up in my room. Said we didn't have to talk about God if I didn't want. He mostly just sat with me. I'd tell him about you guys. He would tell me stories about traveling through Europe on trains. Sometimes he would read to me."

"Sounds romantic," I said.

"He's a very nice man. He told me he prays for me every night."

My father wasn't there, and no one mentioned it.

After dinner Ramona and I watched TV in my bedroom, which was also the attic.

"Where do you think Dad is?" she said.

"Working late."

"Probably."

From my bed, I could hear my mother at the piano. She played Chopin, one of the nocturnes. I imagined the music mixing with all the dust and soot in the pipes as it came up through the grates. By the time it reached me it sounded condensed, congested.

In the middle of the night I woke with the feeling I'd been dreaming the same music that I'd fallen asleep listening to. I looked out the window. My father's car was in the driveway. Beneath the streetlamp, a raccoon was fucking up our garbage.

This was around the time my parents made me start seeing a shrink. His name was Goldstein or Rothstein, something-stein, and I just knew he was an adult version of the type of arrogant shits I went to school with. I lied and told him I didn't do drugs. Dr. -stein didn't believe me. My parents had already told him I did. I could tell he thought I was this typical angsty bourgeois stoner. He wasn't smart enough to understand the depths of my existential suffering.

"You don't get me," I said.

"You have to let me try," he said.

"Whatever," I said. "I think my sister's lezzing it out with your daughter."

He paused. "And how does that make *you* feel?"

"I don't know. She's *your* daughter."

"We're not here to discuss my daughter," he said, though it seemed like he was thinking about it, wondering if it was true. It wasn't. He probably never sees her, I thought. They have their own bathrooms, keep different hours. Sometimes they pass in the kitchen.

"So what do you want to discuss?" I said.

"You," he said, "We're here to discuss you."

"This is bullshit," I said.

My sister was at the movies with Matt Poncett. So she claimed. She was probably blowing him in the front seat of his car, parked sketchily on the top level of the Papa Gino's/Filene's Basement parking garage.

"Eat some peas," my mother said. "You don't eat enough vegetables."

She put some on my plate, and I smushed them with my fork.

"Zach," my father said. He placed his hand on my shoulder. "Are you okay?"

This was code for "Did you just rip a fat blunt of orange-haired beasters?" Or "We know you jizzed all over the Frida Kahlo poster in the upstairs bathroom, but actually it doesn't look half bad now, like your dried come is her tears."

"I'm chill," I said.

"We know you're chill," my mother said. "That's what we're worried about. Sometimes you seem a bit too chill."

"You're going to graduate in a year," my father said. "What do you plan to do after that? With your grades, I'm not sure college will be—"

"Don't say that, Mark . . ." my mother said.

"I'm just saying—" my father said.

"If he gets his grades up—" my mother said.

"I'm just saying it might be time to start thinking—"

"Zach," my mother said, "I know we've been distracted lately. I know we haven't had a lot of time for you. It's been tough with my surgery and everything."

"Whatever," I said.

"Not whatever," my father said.

When my sister got home it was late. I could smell the essence of jizz on her.

"Dad's out again," she said.

"You let him come all over you."

"You're insane."

"Don't you have any dignity?"

"Don't you?"

"No," I said, and ripped a scab off my arm that I'd been picking.

By this point we were deep into April. Spring break was over. I'd spent it in my room playing *GoldenEye* and eating Little Debbie's Zebra Cakes. Through the window I'd watch Ramona run out to Matt Poncett's pickup, holding her jacket over her head so she wouldn't get wet. The door would pop open, and she'd climb in. Her skirt rode up her ass when she made the step up.

An hour or so later my father would walk out to his own car. He didn't appear to notice the rain. I knew my mother was alone downstairs, abandoned by all, listening to the rain like it was a requiem. I couldn't bring myself to walk down and say hello.

But now school was back, and Father Larry was showing up even more often. They'd be in the kitchen every day when I got home.

"You think Mom's fucking the priest?" I asked Ramona. She was standing in the upstairs bathroom with the door open, applying mascara. I lingered, half in the bathroom, half in the hall.

"He's a priest," she said. "He's married to Jesus."

"That's nuns."

"Then who are priests married to?"

"I don't know. I don't think they're married to anyone."

"Maybe the Virgin Mary?"

"What do you know about virgins?" I said.

"I don't," Ramona said. "There's only one virgin in this house. Everyone's getting some but you."

She said it casually, blinking to perfect her lashes.

"I have a girlfriend," I said.

"Sure," Ramona said.

One night at Weinberg's, me, him, and Mike took ecstasy. We sat in his basement and listened to the techno remix of that Rusted Root song with the African drumming. I took off my shirt, rubbed my naked back against the leather recliner. We played *Mario Kart* and chewed gum. We each took a second pill; they were called Mercedes and had the logo imprinted on them. No girls came over. At sunrise we drove down to the lake. Lying in the grass I felt like I was lying in a hammock. I thought about my family and imagined them as pieces of clay that only needed to be fused together and fired in a kiln in order to take a shape and hold it.

We fell asleep outside for a couple hours. We were late for school. Weinberg swung me by my house so I could grab my backpack. My father was at work already. Before I got in I could hear my mother's piano. It was Bach, a piece she used to play for me when I was a kid. Father Larry was sitting in my father's chair, listening. Both their eyes were closed, but sunlight came in the window, and I knew they were seeing bright colors beneath their eyelids.

I stood in the doorway. Father Larry had his legs crossed like he was meditating. A carton of OJ and an empty champagne bottle were on the table. The floor was wet from where the champagne had spilled.

My mother made mistakes but played through, as if they were part of the piece. I grabbed my backpack and left.

At school I could barely stay awake. Matt Poncett was in my Spanish class, and he kept looking at me, smiling. I raised my hand. "Can I go to the nurse?"

"*¡Hable en español!*" Ms. Vasquez said.

I shrugged and put my head on the desk. In the hallway after, Matt Poncett winked at me and said, "*Hola, amigo.*"

When I got home, Father Larry and my mother were napping on the window seat in the living room. They were on their backs, head to toe, legs slightly intertwined. Peter Gabriel sang, "*In your eyes, the light the heat.*"

For a moment I considered curling up between them, resting my head in the nook of my mother's armpit, lulled by the mingling smells of sweat, coffee, and pH-balanced deodorant. Instead, I went up to my room. I turned off all the lights and lay in silence, staring at the glow-in-the-dark stars on my ceiling.

Later, I heard my mother on the phone. I peered through the crack in the door. She wore a bathrobe, paced.

"I'm not even a woman anymore," she said. "There's nothing left for them to remove."

Then there was a long pause, and she stood, looking out the window.

"There's no point in going through it again," she said. "There's nothing left."

At dinner, no one was hungry.

"How was your day?" my father said.

Ramona shrugged. I could tell she'd been crying because she wasn't wearing makeup. She always wore makeup, even to field hockey. She only took it off when she'd been crying.

"What's the matter with you?" I said to Ramona.

"I'm full," she said. "I'm going upstairs."

I was playing *GoldenEye* when my father came up to my room. I didn't turn around, but I knew it was him from the way he took the stairs, slower than the others, probably planning exactly what to say.

He came right in and sat next to me on the edge of the waterbed. I kept playing my game.

"Can I play with you?"

"If you want." He picked up the second controller. "LTK. License to kill. One shot and you're dead. You can be Bond."

"What are the buttons?"

"Z shoots, yellow buttons walk sideways, down yellow and R-button ducks, B switches weapons, the joystick adjusts the sight when you have the sniper rifle. Hold down and the R-button at the same time to zoom in."

"I'll figure it out," he said.

We played in the Temple level. I took three shots at him with a Cougar Magnum from behind a pillar, but he managed to duck out of the way. He threw a grenade, and I had to scurry backwards.

"Your mother," he said.

"What about her?"

"She's sick again."

I picked up a rocket launcher, headed up the stairs. I could see on my father's side of the screen that all he had was a throwing knife.

"I know," I said. "I heard her on the phone. I think she was talking to her spiritual adviser."

"Father Larry."

"The one and only."

I launched a rocket, but I was too far away and missed him completely. He disappeared out of sight. He had a sniper rifle now, and I didn't know where he was going.

"What's gonna happen?" I said.

"I don't know."

"It's bad, right?"

"It's not good."

I walked back down the stairs looking for him. It was already too late when I saw him aim at me from above. One shot from the sniper rifle, and I was done. My screen filled with blood.

"You learn fast," I said. My father put down his controller. His hands were shaking like he'd really shot me.

"It's best of five," I said.

"I have to do some work," he said, and left me there. I sat by the window and watched for his car to leave. It stayed put that night.

The next morning Ramona said she was sick and didn't get out of bed, so I went to school without her. When I got there, everyone knew except me. Apparently he'd shown the tape to his brother, who'd made copies and distributed it to a bunch of sophomores. There'd been a screening at Joe Bort's house on his big TV.

"Why does everyone keep looking at me weird?" I said to Weinberg.

"You don't know?"

"Know what?"

"Your sister made a sex tape with Matt Poncett. Everyone's seen it."

"What the fuck?"

"There's supposed to be some kinky shit on there."

"We got to get a copy of that tape," Mike said.

I punched him on the arm.

"That's my sister, you douche."

"I heard she deep-throats him," Weinberg said.

"That's not kinky," Mike said. "Impressive, but not really kinky."

"There's other stuff too," Weinberg said. "She's wearing her cheerleader outfit."

"I heard he's hung like Mark Wahlberg," Mike said.

"I don't want to hear about it," I said.

"It's not really his dick in the movie," Weinberg said. "They used a prosthetic."

Ramona was in her room and wouldn't come out. My mother was in the hallway, pleading at the door. Father Larry sat silent on the stairs.

"Just talk to me, Ramona," my mother said. "That's all I ask."

Ramona didn't reply, but we could hear her crying.

"She's been crying all day," my mother said.

"It's okay to be angry," my mother said to the door. "Anger is a healthy stage of grief. I'm angry myself. But maybe if we talk about it we can start to come to terms with it."

"I don't think that's what she's upset about," I said.

"Of course that's what she's upset about," my mother said.

Ramona yelled something. It sounded like "Go away," but you couldn't really tell.

My mother turned to the priest. "You try to talk to her. Maybe she'll listen to you. You're so good at this type of thing."

"That might not be the best idea," I said.

Father Larry stood up. When he opened her door, she started shrieking.

"Get the fuck out," she yelled.

Father Larry walked in and shut the door behind him. The shrieking continued.

When he came out he said, "I don't think she wants to talk to me right now. Sometimes you have to give a person space to make peace on their own."

The shrieking went back to being sobbing.

"I can't bear this," my mother said. "You try, Zach. Try to talk to her. She looks up to you."

"She doesn't look up to me."

"She does," Father Larry said.

"How do you know?"

"You're her big brother."

"So?"

"Just try," my mother said.

"Leave her alone," I said, and went up to my room.

Eventually my mother stopped banging on Ramona's door. She and the priest were probably in the living room. He let her cry into his palm. He told her about Job, about Jesus.

When my father came home, Ramona wouldn't talk to him either. She didn't come down for dinner. The priest was still there, and we had pizza. Father Larry took the last slice of sausage and pepperoni. "You guys can't eat pork anyway," Father Larry said.

"We don't keep kosher," I said.

"Maybe we should," my father said. "Maybe then God would like us more." I couldn't tell if he was joking or not.

"I'll bring a couple slices up and see if Ramona wants any," I said.

She didn't answer when I knocked, so I opened the door and let myself in. I didn't see her at first. She lay on the floor behind her bed with her legs together and straight ahead, arms folded across her chest. She wore a frilly nightgown that I hadn't seen in ages, since before she got breasts, legs. It was only a few years ago that she was a kid, that we both were.

"Hey," I said. I put the plate of pizza on her desk. She wasn't crying anymore, just staring at the ceiling.

"I'm not hungry."

"I'll eat it if you don't want it."

"Do whatever you want," she said. I took a bite.

"I assume you heard," she said.

"I heard."

I had been planning to give her a piece of my mind, let her know how embarrassing this was for me, how stupid she'd been. But looking at her on the floor in that nightgown I couldn't.

"Everyone will forget about it by tomorrow," I said.

"They won't."

I leaned against her bed. Her phone vibrated.

"You gonna get that?"

"Leave it."

"You know what the good thing about high school is?" I said.

"What?"

"It's only four years. Then it's over."

She didn't say anything.

"You only have two years left," I said. "And it's almost summer. Everyone will go away and forget all about you."

Ramona started crying again.

"It'll be okay," I said. I knew she knew I didn't mean it, but I said it anyway, and she let me say it. "It will all be okay," I said.

Father Larry was over every day now. He'd be there in the morning when I woke up. He made the coffee, burnt the toast. He always had the Sports section, so I'd read the Living/Arts instead. You couldn't say anything because my mother was right there. She was going to die soon; you weren't allowed to complain. No one said this specifically, but we all knew. Ramona even went back to school.

People called her Deep Throat behind her back, and sometimes to her face; they called her Ramona Jameson, Ramona Does Dallas. If I were at all tough I would have punched a few lights out, but I wasn't, so I didn't. I mostly stopped going to classes and got high in the woods or in Weinberg's Jetta. I knew Mike had a copy of the tape.

I'd stopped masturbating entirely. Every time I started I would picture Ramona getting it from behind in her cheerleader outfit. In my head, she would be crying, makeup dripping like blue paint onto the floor, spreading all over the walls and ceiling, tinting everything deep blue, so blue it was almost black.

In real life, she seemed to be handling it okay. She got new friends, bad-girl friends. She was a celebrity. She got to be Lady Macbeth in the school play; everyone said she was right for the part.

I didn't have much interaction with Ramona or any of them. My mother was busy meditating with her priest, reading poems about ficus trees, telling herself that every living thing dies. She wore Indian saris, and in the evenings she would burn incense. She'd been losing weight. It mostly showed in her face.

One night she came to my room and looked like she was about to say something important, but she just said, "Zachary," as if it were not yet my name but still a single sperm that had spilled from my father's body into hers and rattled around like a pinball, or a recurring dream, before settling into that place she no longer had, growing slowly and deliberately of its own accord.

Father Larry gave her a cross. She wore it on a chain around her neck that also had a Star of David and a tiny amethyst. Father Larry held her hand; I was glad he was there. I didn't know what happened when he was gone, when I went upstairs and my parents were alone together in their bedroom.

At some point, my father returned to his nighttime excursions. He'd stopped for a couple weeks after my mother's news, but it didn't take him long to get back to it. Things seemed close to normal. Ramona got a new boyfriend. He was one of the popular kids.

One night, I picked Ramona up from play practice. It was May now, and the stars were almost as bright as the glow-in-the-dark ones on my ceiling. With the window open, you could smell charcoal and propane. The air smelled like baseball; it smelled like what I imagined sex would smell like. I didn't ask Ramona if I was right.

We drove through the center of town, past the ice-cream place and the local sports bar. On benches outside the former, middle schoolers sat in gender-segregated groups. They pushed hair from their eyes, inched toward each other like weak magnets. Behind a streetlamp, brave tongues danced beginner's tangos, shyly at first, gradually growing comfortable, learning to dip and dash, braces clinking and scraping like braking trains.

Next door, on the patio, men loosened ties, wiped frost from their mouths. They held cigarettes at arm's length so their wives wouldn't smell it on them. I imagined Ramona was watching them out the window, wondering if her husband would be the same, or if she'd ever have one.

"How's the play going?" I said.

"It's whatever," she said.

We were coming to our street. As I turned the corner I saw my father's car zip off in the other direction.

"Where do you think he goes?" Ramona said.

"Let's find out. I've seen how they do it in movies. You just have to stay two car lengths behind."

"He's getting on the highway," Ramona said.

We passed a string of side-of-the-road motels. I kept expecting him to pull into one, into a space he knew by heart. Ramona and I would linger in the shadows. A door would fly open. A woman would be standing there, eyes alight, silk robe slipping open. My father would approach; the woman would take him in her arms like he was a lost child. They'd disappear into the room. The blinds would close.

He kept driving. I followed.

"He's getting off," I said. We were in Waltham. We got on another, smaller highway heading toward Lexington. In the distance I could see Wal-Lex, a rollerskating rink. Everyone used to have birthday parties there when we were kids. It looked open. I wondered if they got a big nighttime crowd, nostalgic adults skating two by two.

My father signaled and pulled into the Wal-Lex lot.

"Dad's going rollerskating?" Ramona said.

"Maybe he's meeting someone here."

When we got inside it was pretty empty. There was a lone skater, a woman in a low-cut black cocktail dress. At a table, a chubby guy ate pizza and watched her. Everything looked smaller than I remembered.

"Over there," Ramona said. She was pointing to the arcade area. "I think I just saw him go that way."

We walked over cautiously, stopping behind a pinball machine to peer out at him. He stood at one of the games. I think it was *Street Fighter II*. From his pocket he pulled rolls of quarters. He rested them in the nook between the screen and joystick.

Dad inserted coins and began to play. His hands moved across the buttons carefully, not desperately like most people's do. He played the way he stood in the rain, with a focused intensity, unaware of his surroundings, gazing deeply at the pixilated men who tore at each other's bodies like crazed dancers or violent lovers.

On the day of the funeral I brought tulips from the front garden to put on the grave, but by the time we got to the cemetery they had already wilted. Everyone was there: cousins, aunts, uncles. The usual people said the usual things. "She was so young," they said.

Ramona stood next to me wearing sunglasses and a black dress. Her hair was pulled back, jet-black. She looked like a young wife at a Mafia funeral. My father flanked me on the other side. He kept his eyes closed the whole time. I thought: this is my family now, we are three now, we wear sunglasses, we close our eyes.

Father Larry spoke. He said she had a big soul; it was too big for her body, for this earth. When he said it I looked straight at the sun to see if it would make me blind.

TELL ME

People from the halfway house come into the store. One guy in particular. I think his name is Richard. He never buys books.

"I came in with this," he says, raises a paperback like Moses with the commandments.

Richard thinks he's funny. He's funnier than the other methadone addicts, who aren't even a little funny. The house is truly halfway: five blocks east to landscaped lawns, five west to boarded-up brownstones. People say they like this city's slippery thresholds, the way the neighborhoods bleed into one another. Those who say they like it live far from the bleeding.

I say, "You."

"This guy," he says.

"You," I say.

"I never buy books. Don't know why I'm always coming in here."

"For the conversation?"

"What conversation?" he says, which makes me sad.

Molly and I are a thing again. That's what my sister calls it. A thing. Sounds like some kind of swamp monster. All it means is I'm back to bringing Molly home for holidays.

Molly doesn't like that I'm always almost asleep. I don't like being woken.

"Are you . . . ?"

"I'll keep watching."

"I don't want to watch if you're asleep."

How to explain the peace I get, TV on, this drift, curled into armpit?

"Don't leave me alone," she says.

There are other things Molly doesn't like about me.

Her roommate, Chandra, goes by Chan, pronounced Sean. Sexy, considering Sean swigs bottled beer, belches, ashes into teacups. You aren't supposed to smoke in the living room. I'm not supposed to smoke ever.

"Women," Sean says.

"Bitches," Sean says.

Richard's indented the leather recliner. He's in the indentation, eyes closed.

"I'm not asleep," he says. "I hear every word you're saying."

"What am I saying?"

"I know even if you're not saying it. You're thinking it."

One thing Molly doesn't like is the six months we weren't a thing. More specifically, she doesn't like the other, almost-thing I was involved in. More specifically, she doesn't like Janine.

I meet Sean at Boat, a bar decorated in boat corpse. Sean likes the word *pussy*. She talks about getting it, then describes some she's seen. The ones she describes don't sound like any I've encountered.

My cell's upset with texts. My head's on the table. Before I know it Sean's pulling my bicep—sneaking a comparative assessment—directing me through traffic to Molly's bed.

"What did I say?" I say.

When I wake Molly's hooked in with headphones, watching murder on her laptop.

I write a note, forget the spelling of Chan. "SEAN—HAVE YOU SEEN MY WALLET?"

All these books are an avalanche in waiting. I want to pile them, climb, collapse, settle among the debris. Most of the time I want to sit down, which isn't allowed. It's not that the job makes me tired so much as it never forces me into full cognition. Richard thinks he's psychic.

"I can tell what everyone's thinking about me."

"There's some old umbrellas in back," I say, because Richard's shirt is soaked.

Saturated. My sweat smells like coffee. Molly says, "What kind of person names their kid Janine?"

Because Janine was in the bodega, bending for our benefit. But it's more than that: Janine's an easy name for an emptiness we can't articulate.

"David Bowie fans?"

"I wasn't asking," she says. The awning isn't enough. Rain falls on our outstretched feet.

"Break's over," I say, cheek-peck, stand, turn, barrel into halogen, situate. Molly walks away, wet. Janine had Molly in the ergonomics department but was mostly a mess. She said it felt metallic, like I was infusing her with lead.

My wallet appears in the lost and found, still empty of money. Note taped to it says, "Thanks for nothing." When it feels like I'm about to fall over I pluck chest hairs. Customers can't believe we don't have what will fix their lives.

"It's been out of print since '86," I say.

"But this is a bookstore."

April ends at night. The barking dogs are beautiful again. Molly has her thumb and index around the base of my neck, stroking. I say, "Shit," meaning, "I'm awake."

Because: The frequency with which she reaches under my shirt, circles my nipples with the bitten ends of fingernails. The way she says the word *orange* like it's two words, "or unge?" The way she slices them into slim eighths, sucks the skins. Looks like she's wearing a mouth guard. The way she still blushes when I look at her breasts.

Rain returns, May begins, we're running.

Collapse into shower, bumping bone, bruising, singing (sort of). I want to rise out of my asshole self, become some sweet specter, line Molly's insides. The closest we come to saying I love you is "Baby, that feels good."

Another time, to test him, I say, "What am I thinking right now?"

"You're thinking I wish this boobjob would get out of my store."

"Boobjob?"

Richard's head is sparsely populated with hair like fish skin, silverish. The way hair gets before it gets going. I'm noticing new features on him always. Maybe it's the program working, buffing, bringing out his shine.

He says, "Used to be my job, anyway."

Janine kept me awake by making me wonder where she was.

Sean's girlfriend's skin's so pink I want to twist her wrist, hear her howl. The state of California's inked into her arm. A reminder of home or the expression of a mind-set. Sean and I stop going to Boat Bar. Sean and Alice stand in the kitchen linked, ashing in the sink, elbowing each other in their taped-down tits, dimple-grinning, perched over our lifestyle, some advanced species of lover. Molly writes "Molly" on her carton of soy milk.

Other guys from the halfway house come in, women too. Haircuts from the wrong decade. Like one decade off from the one in fashion. They're careful not to bend the pages. Everyone wants the same book about the 2012 apocalypse. That or chess strategy.

"Where's Richard?" I ask. "Has anyone seen Richard?"

No one knows who I'm talking about.

"You and your Mayans," I say to no one.

Molly still says it feels good, but spring is short and summer snakes up, sticks out its tongue, turns down our volume. We listen to Sean smacking Alice, saying, "Yeah," saying, "You lying bitch," saying, "Jesus, baby, Jesus." Alice yells, "Tell me," at what might be the moment of climax. When Alice's head hits hardwood, Molly calls. Cops arrive, chub-cheeked, straight from a paperback. They pull everyone apart. I'm the only one not crying. I feel like the culprit. Two hours later it's hard to tell who's doing what to whom, or if it's in the right spirit, until someone says, "I think I'm gonna."

"How can you sleep?" Molly says, turns the TV up.

With us it's different. We check e-mail immediately after.

Business is moderate, which seems like a miracle to everyone but the owners. A customer tells me coffee stops working after a while. Molly stops meeting me on my lunch breaks.

But one night: Me, Molly, Sean on the roof, hitting beer cans with a Wiffle bat. "Bottom of the ninth," I say, meaning, "Sometimes we come so close."

The problem is the space between what we want to feel and what we've come to expect from certain situations. Sometimes I think that space is what it means to be an adult.

Then, desperate to dry, Molly pulls on a Janine-dress found in my closet, beige cotton, floral print, scoop neck. "My sister must have left it," I say. And try to smell something foreign as she climbs atop me.

Dress back up. For a moment it's a lampshade; her head the hidden bulb, body a decorative base.

Meanwhile, Alice is out, Erica's in, Sean has started a band, Clit Pincher. The logo is a lobster claw. Their only song: "Alice."

Molly's mom keeps asking Molly if she's happy. Molly

keeps asking me what she should tell her mom. I say, "Baby, I'm tired. Can we talk in the morning?"

Richard isn't dead, but he has found Jesus. He's hawking crosses by the corner of Court and Pacific.

"What you think is the bleak shit," he tells me, "isn't always the bleak shit."

Eventually it's cold again. Restraining orders expire. Alice returns, sings her usual. They start slow, so I imagine, work themselves over each other, into each other, up to speed.

"Tell me! Tell me, Sean!"

We all await a response.

SLUTS AT HEART

The country was voting Young vs. Vegas Elvis for the national stamp. The West Coast was in flames over Rodney King. George Bush had ten points in the polls on Bill Clinton, with third-party lunatic Ross Perot loudly gaining steam. My friend Simit was dying.

I did what anyone would do; I bought a kitten. She was an ill-tempered, whimpering thing I called Lisa Marie. Lisa Marie proceeded to fight it out with human Lisa for my affection. During sex, Lisa Marie would attach herself to the fleshy part of Lisa's calf and bite.

On the one hand you had Young Elvis, in a sport coat and a smile. He had cheekbones to die for, piercing baby blues. A single strand of hair dangled down his forehead like Superman's coiffed *S*. The other option was Vegas, gold stars stitched to popped collar, brows low over eyes. Clinton had come out in support of Young. What I couldn't figure was who was voting for Vegas. Showgirls? Seventies nostalgics? Doomers?

"I like Vegas Elvis," Lisa said.

We were cooking for Maggie and Sam. Eggplant stew. Maggie and Sam were on the Himmler-Goebbels diet—no meat, nuts, or anything on the red-green color spectrum. They were the type of couple who tried new things: taking salsa dance classes, aging their own cheese. Lisa and I were the type of couple who made fun of couples who tried new things. Maybe we were envious.

"What do you mean you like Vegas Elvis?" I said.

"I don't know. I just like him. He seems more human or something. Like, you know he's gonna drop dead next time he sits on the toilet."

"And that should be on a postage stamp?"

"I'm just saying," she said.

"What are you just saying?"

"I'm just saying if there was a vote, I might choose Vegas Elvis, yes."

"But there is a vote," I said.

Lisa grabbed an orange from the counter, weighed it in her palm, threatened to throw it at me, put it down. The orange rolled to the floor. Lisa Marie lapped its skin.

"I'm not really much of a voter," Lisa said.

The way she said it made me think of an article I'd read about our generation's apathy.

Maggie and Sam brought wine—white wine with no nuts in it. I would have made a joke, but it was the year of people not making jokes. After half a decade taking ecstasy on roof decks and debating brands of cereal, our lives had taken a turn toward the serious. Everyone we knew was getting married, including Maggie and Sam. The true artists among us had either found success or accepted some level of prolonged poverty. The others were going corporate or applying to law school. My old pal from high school had terminal cancer, and I was too scared to discuss it. I felt angry and took my anger out on Lisa. She was the nearest one at hand.

The stew was limp and viscous, but with enough Tabasco you could make it taste like Tabasco. Sam went for seconds, then thirds. We were a couple bottles of deep when Lisa got the whiskey out of the cabinet. She poured it straight into our wineglasses. The talking got on to sexiness.

"What I find sexy," I said, "are sluts."

My girlfriend glared.

"Hear me out," I said. There was something I was trying to get at. It had to do with Simit.

"I'm not talking about sluts in practice. I'm talking about sluts deep down. Sluts at heart."

"How poetic," Lisa said.

"Just listen for a second," I said, though I wasn't sure what came next. Maybe *sluts* was the wrong word. "What I mean is someone who lives without fear of the consequences of her actions."

Maggie and Sam looked at each other.

"I don't get it," Maggie said.

Sam knew enough to keep his mouth shut.

"He has a thing for cutoff denim skirts," Lisa said. "That's all he means. He's always trying to get me to wear them."

"Unrelated," I said. There was a clichéd image of rural America that invaded my fantasies: some farmer's daughter, foreign to my New York life. I'd work in the fields, too worn out for anxiety.

"Can men be sluts at heart?" Maggie said.

"All men are sluts at heart," Sam said.

Lisa lifted an eyebrow, raised her glass.

"That not what I mean," I said. "Forget sluts for a minute. Tattoos are sexy. Can we agree on that?"

Lisa had a tattoo, so this was an okay thing to say. She was proud of the tattoo, wore halter tops to show it off.

"Definitely sexy," Maggie said. She winked at Lisa.

"But why?" I said. "Why is it that we find tattoos sexy?"

"Enlighten us," Lisa said, rolled her eyes.

"The bad boy thing," Maggie said. "It's that whole bad-boy thing. Tattoos, cigarettes, beer, and motorcycles. Like James Dean. That shit is sexy. Rock and fucking roll, you know?"

"Or like Elvis," I said.

"James Dean didn't have a tattoo," Sam said. He was a stickler for facts. "And neither, for that matter, did your man the King."

"Whatever," Maggie said. "He had all the other things."

"But this is my point," I said. "These things all have something in common: consequences. To do these things you must ignore consequences. A tattoo, for example. You can't get a tattoo unless you ignore the fact that one day you'll be old and it will be wrinkled on loose skin, and that you'll be sick of your shamrock or mom heart or whatever you decided to get for eternity. And think of that word, *eternity*. Everyone knows tattoos are permanent, right? Bullshit. They're not permanent. By pretending they're permanent we're pretending our bodies are permanent. That's what's sexy. It's like driving a motorcycle—to ride one you have to convince yourself that you're not gonna snap your head off."

"Motorcycles aren't sexy," Lisa said.

"Bullshit, motorcycles aren't sexy," I said.

"They're not," Lisa said. "People who ride them are stupid. Everyone I've ever known who had one has been in an accident."

By everyone, she meant her uncle Phil, a mustached Arizonan who'd lost what few brain cells he'd had doing daredevil shit.

"It's retarded," Lisa said.

"A retarded way to become retarded," Sam said.

"That's not nice," Maggie said. She had a retarded cousin.

The rest of the night went badly. Maggie and Sam left. There was a discussion, which led to another discussion. Eventually it came out that Lisa had found naked pictures of my ex-girlfriend from college.

"Why didn't you throw them out?"

"I'll throw them out," I said.

"That's not the point," Lisa said. " I want you to want to throw them out."

Sometimes, when Lisa and I had sex, we'd lock the cat in the bathroom. We could hear her clawing at the door. It added a measure of intensity to the act. After, as we lay entwined, Lisa Marie would lick the salt off my skin.

But I should tell about Simit. By the time they found the tumors they were everywhere: liver, lungs, pancreas. I hadn't visited or even talked to him. It had been a few years.

One weekend I drove up to Boston with Ava, another old friend, to attend a fundraiser for a nonprofit organization Simit had started.

Simit was a good person. He could also be kind of a dick. Ava was named after the actress Ava Gardner, who, from what I've read, was a slut both in practice and at heart.

Lisa was not a fan of Ava. She was jealous, I think, of the fact that I'd known Ava longer. There were parts of my life that Ava had access to and Lisa did not. People often asked when Lisa and I were going to get engaged. We would look at each other as if the other might have the answer.

Marrying seemed like the right move—we'd lived together for four years already and loved each other—but something held us back. Maybe it was the finality of it, concession to a lifetime of low-pulse domesticity. Not that there was anything wrong with what we had. But we were foolish romantics holding out hope for soul mates—we'd watched too many rom-coms.

In the past, I had entertained the thought that Ava could be that soul mate. Lisa sensed this—another reason why they didn't get along. Ava and I would have made a terrible couple, I'm sure. But the fact that we'd never attempted it charged our friendship with an unspoken air of possibility. I didn't intend to act on those feelings, but there was that underlying want: to check another box, check into another body, fold yourselves into what might, this time, make a whole.

On the car ride, I told Ava things about my life that made me sound more bohemian than I actually was. I wrote radio ads for a car dealership. I pretended it was to support myself while I worked on my screenplay, but I just liked saying "my screenplay." It made me sound like I had ambition, but also, in retrospect, like a douche bag.

We talked about Simit. We were both scared to see him. Ava was scared that she would cry. I was scared that I would remember that I would one day die, that Ava would, that Lisa would. Simit was always trying to get me to do something with my life. By something he meant a job where I wouldn't make money but would feel better about myself as a person.

The fundraiser was at a warehouse in a suburb north of Boston. A company called Don't Worry Be Hippy sold overstock at outlet prices. A percentage of the proceeds would go to Simit's nonprofit, a group he'd founded that did outreach at local homeless shelters. Mostly it was T-shirts with peace signs on them. A fiver got you thirty bucks of retail. Bargain hunters were out in droves.

Don't Worry Be Hippy had hired teenagers to wear jester outfits and spread cheer. They banged bongo drums. One of the T-shirts had a picture of a leaping dolphin. It said "The Best Ism is Optimism."

We found Simit handshaking in a corner. When his mom saw us she cried. We'd hung around their house a lot when we were younger. It must have felt like "Kavya Bose, this is your life!" Simit ignored his mother.

"Whatup?" he said.

Simit looked sick. More so, he looked homeless. He'd always carried an air of homelessness—wispy goatee, Chiahair, a preference for thrift-shop men's formal wear—but it was offset by broad shoulders and a sated, healthy gut. Now he looked like he could be selling incense on a street corner.

In place of hair stood an L.A. Raiders cap, worn in solidarity with the Rodney King rioters. When I hugged him he said, "Look at you, all big and shit."

Simit had slept with Ava once, in her anorexic years, a long span. Ava often alluded to this period of her life, but it was not openly discussed. I'd always hoped she would confide in me. I wanted to be someone people came to with their problems. Lisa bottled hers up, spilled only to her shrink. I was the same.

"Ave," Simit said. "You look beautiful."

"Thanks," she said.

"Your breasts," he said. "Bigger?"

This was the wrong thing to say, what with his mom standing right there and it being the year of people not making jokes.

"I don't think so," Ava said.

"Birth control?" Simit said.

He reminded me of Simit, the one I'd known in seventh grade, before he became a good person, when we used to watch porn in his basement.

Ava said his penis was huge. It was huge. I'd seen it once, accidentally, after swimming. When he saw me looking he said, "Yours will get bigger too one day." We were twenty-five at the time.

Simit had people to talk to: cousins who'd driven from the Cape, some guy in a leather jacket. I thought the guy might be his father, who I hadn't seen since fourth grade, but who I'd heard was back.

Ava and I walked around. We drank the complimentary coffee. I bought a T-shirt for my mom. The shirt said "Earth Mother." She would never wear it. Ava bought twelve T-shirts, fleece slippers, and a tote bag. Her parents had given her the money.

Before leaving, Simit patted Ava's butt. I think he was hoping for a pity fuck. Maybe just a pity blow job. Later, he told me he'd have settled for a pity hand job. I guess that's a more common thing.

I thought that when he was dead I'd remember this and say, "He was horny right to the end. As his body failed, his inner life was strong and pervy." Whoever I was with would say, "I'm so sorry."

We went to Simit's mom's apartment, where he'd been living since the diagnosis. The leather jacket guy came too. He was actually an uncle. The real father was back, but only on Tuesdays and Wednesdays.

We sat around a giant TV Simit had bought when he found out he was dying. "I got a gift certificate," he said.

Baseball was on. The Red Sox were losing. Simit fell asleep. His mom brought out tea. There was a kid imitating batting stances, a cousin. He was pretty good: Greenwell, Boggs.

I wanted us to be cheerful. I wanted Simit to be cheered. We watched TV with the volume down.

"C'mere baby," Ava said to the dog.

I helped Kavya with the dishes. There was a piece of tomato that wouldn't come off the plate. I picked with my fingernail, but Kavya grabbed my wrist. I dropped the plate and it broke in the sink.

"Leave it," she said.

I opened the fridge for no reason and then closed it. We brought out dessert.

Simit woke up. Chocolate was one of the few things he could digest. First he smoked a joint.

"This is good, mom," he said.

"Delicious," Ava said.

Simit was eyeing her. "So what's the deal? It's been a while. New York, right?"

"I got a cat," I said. "And a girlfriend."

He was still the guy who wanted me to do something with my life, the one who held his sexual experiences over my head.

"Lisa," I said. "They're both named Lisa. The lovely Lisas."

"All grown up now," Simit said. "You want a prize?"

"You fucker," I said.

The uncle gave me a look. The kid was playing Game Boy. He hadn't heard the swear.

"How's that screenplay?" Simit said in a tone suggesting—rightly—that no such screenplay existed.

"Actually, it's going well."

"Oh, really?" Ava said.

"What's it about, then?" Simit said.

"Yeah, tell us," Ava said.

"It's about this guy, a young guy. He's a college gradu- ate, but he's broke, so he starts begging for change. But he has to put mud on his face and stuff. To look homeless. But then he meets this girl . . ."

"Yeah, yeah," Simit said. "I already saw that movie. There's an acoustic guitar. He gets the girl in the end." He was smiling.

Ava laughed.

"Did I not mention that I have a girlfriend, assholes?" I said.

"And a cat too," Simit said. "What a guy." The laughter continued.

Simit said he wanted to hear about Ava. What he really wanted was to hear about the old days. We talked about the old days.

"You look good," Simit said to Ava. Actually, he looked good. Or better than he had before the joint. He was playing the version of himself I would miss the most— ruthlessly truthful, but without animosity. Simit exuded warmth even when he was giving you a hard time.

"You used to be a big girl. Then you got real skinny. Too skinny. When was that?"

"High school," Ava said. "And college."

"You're perfect now. With hips." His voice sounded wistful.

"Thanks," Ava said.

Simit and I went out for air. The balcony overlooked a parking lot, cars glowing, sunset desolidifying. Simit lit a cigarette.

"What could it hurt?" he said.

I thought of Vegas Elvis, his descent into gluttony; the way you never see his eyes in the pictures from that era; those last performances of Sinatra's "My Way," all garbled and almost-great, floppy with bathos, but unforgivably loveless.

"You voting for the stamp?" I said.

"What stamp?"

"The Elvis stamp."

"Fuck Elvis," Simit said. "He stole it all from my niggas."

"You can't say niggas," I said. "You're Indian."

"I have cancer," he said. "I can say what I want."

"Okay," I said.

Through the window we saw Ava get frisky with the dog. She stroked its belly, held a hand around its scruff. The cousin had fallen asleep in his father's arms. It looked like an advertisement. There was an advertisement on the TV. It was one I'd seen a thousand times. For tires, local, complete with poor production and laughably thick Boston accents. The type of commercial that's annoying until you live somewhere else, and then you kind of miss it.

"You can fuck her when I'm dead," Simit said.

I paused too long before laughing.

"Bag that," Simit said. "She won't let you fuck her until she's dead."

"I'm into that," I said. "Dead chicks."

"I'll send some your way," Simit said.

Back home, things were happening. Lisa Marie had eaten a condom in my absence, been rushed to the animal ER. The condom was caught in the cat's small intestine. I went straight there, met Lisa in the waiting room. The waiting room was filled with high-def photos of beautiful dogs. A man sat in the corner cradling an iguana, speaking to it in a baby voice.

Lisa Marie died on the operating table. Lisa couldn't look, but I held the cat's limp body, stroked her fur like she could still feel it. Her body was cold. I touched her teeth.

Lisa attributed the condom to Maggie and Sam, but I didn't buy it. Why would Maggie and Sam be having sex at our apartment? I asked if she'd seen that guy from her office, Mike or whatever his name was. "His name's Mitch," Lisa said.

Months later. On the Union Square steps were two Elvis impersonators. One was Latino with a mustache and a pretty gold tooth. Junk scars on his arms. The other was Elvis if he'd lived, fallen further. Guitar painted like an American flag. I put in a buck, watched for a while. They did a pretty good "All Shook Up." Tourists took pictures. A blond girl came over, danced a loose-limbed shuffle. Her skirt was filthy white, ripped around the knees. She had a pretty smile, the kind that seems so natural that you wonder what she's hiding. I gave her a look that tried to be love. It came out more like *Love me in a toilet stall?* She told me to fuck off.

Young Elvis won in a landslide, stuck himself squarely to our envelopes. He traversed the country on trucks and trains, like the ones he used to sing about. Attendance at Graceland rose for a while and then dipped back to normal.

AMERICA IS ME AND ANDY

'm done being friends with dreadlocked white guys. But try telling Andy, the only person ever to make a homosexual pass at me. In fairness to Andy, it was Halloween, I was dressed as Lara Croft, and I do have slim wrists and a thin waist since I got that Adderall prescription and stopped eating.

"Is it because I tried to make out with you?" Andy says.

We sit on the futon in his parents' basement watching the audition round of *American Idol*. Knotty hair covers the hurt in his eyes.

"You've known me for, what, ten years?" I say to Andy.

"About," he says.

I say, "And you really think I'm a homophobe? That's what you really think?"

"I dunno," Andy says in that nonconfrontational way that warms my soul but also feels like the kind of weakness that doesn't work in this cruel world.

"Well, let me ask you: if I'm so uncomfortable with gender-role reversal and nontraditional forms of erotic fantasy, then how come I was able to dress up as Lara Croft in the first place?"

"I don't know," Andy says. "But I still think it's because I tried to make out with you."

"Don't be narcissistic," I say. "It's not just you. I'm getting rid of all my white friends with dreadlocks."

"What other ones?"

"Well, there aren't really any others at the present moment, but I think you're missing the big picture here. It's more the principle of it, if anything. It's about growing up, Andy. It's about reaching my full potential as a red-blooded college-educated suburban male."

"You never finished college."

"That's exactly my point. I never finished college because I was hanging out with white people with dreadlocks."

"You mean me?"

"I mean whoever."

Andy is stumped, offended, already over it. He retreats into his cell phone.

The commercial is over. Ryan Seacrest says, "You did it, America. Your votes propelled Lee DeWyze to the top. Soon you'll have a chance to pick another lucky winner."

The way he says it makes it sound like America is one guy, some schmuck in a living room in Des Moines.

But maybe America is me and Andy.

Shitty singers sing. It's unclear if the shittiness is an act or if they're deluded, drunk on ephemeral fame. Andy is texting.

"Who you texting?"

"None of your business."

"New gay friend?"

"Yes, new gay friend."

"When you gonna introduce me?

"He has dreadlocks," Andy says.

Andy balls his hairy hands into hairy fists. Like the kind of lion cub who's cute until he kills you. I feel a tenderness toward him. I want to reach over with scissors, trim his smelly head-pubes, show him what it means to be alive. We watch a commercial for Ford trucks.

Now a blonde sings syrupy shit. The kind of blonde who would never fuck the kind of guy I am. From the Midwest, believes in Jesus, saving herself for someone who can share her soul via social media. Her voice: heartbreakingly mediocre. I want to lick every inch with my ugly tongue. Lick her armpits.

Then a muumuu-ed redhead, made up like a circus clown.

Andy turns to me, eyebrows raised in a gesture of our old camaraderie. Let us bond, he seems to say, in this other human's shame. Let us be brave enough to engage in this ugliness.

The girl's voice is actually good. She sings Aretha, transcends herself. "Ain't No Way."

Moments like these—Apple pie, baseball—are why we fight wars.

Next thing I know Andy's cock's in my mouth, and I'm sucking with every atom, salivating. Our girl belts the blues. I think I am crying.

My mother comes down the stairs. I see her. She sees Andy's acned ass and the silhouette of my soul, mid-cock-suck. The look on her face is called "Baby, I birthed you / Babe, I endorsed you / Watch as we both burn to ash."

I bite Andy's cock. Andy's scream coincides with a cheer from the *Idol* audience. Ryan Seacrest is smiling somewhere. There's blood on my face. Mom walks back up the stairs. But I won't forget that look. It's the look we give for the rest of our lives.

WHAT'S IMPORTANT IS FEELING

We'd been shooting for two weeks already, melting. Most of the crew had chiggers bad. Chiggers, we were told, crawl in and lay eggs beneath your skin. They attack ankles and genitals. The cure is nail polish. A good coating will smother them to death. We wore the clear stuff so it wouldn't show.

Only the L.A. people got them. The Texans wore sulfur in their socks to keep the chiggers out. They didn't mention this trick to us. Nathaniel and I sat on our opposing motel beds—A/C on, anchorman singing box scores in soothing Texas twang—examining the bumps around our sock and jock lines. My body was a morgue; chigger corpses floated through my veins, suffocated under my skin.

"Tonight I plan to dream about Monica Bradley," said Nathaniel. "Her dream self will meet my dream self somewhere in the depths of my unconscious, and we'll talk until sunrise."

Monica was the film's female lead. Older than us, but looked five years younger with non-hips and blond fuzz on her pale arms. Monica's character was meant to be seventeen. There was something deeply erotic in the way her smoke-seasoned voice slipped into teenybop squawk-talk when the cameras came on.

"She's sexy," I said. "Definitely."

"But her personality, I mean. She's great, right? That joke she told about her mom and the albino. Was that a joke? It might have been a true story. Man, what an interesting life."

I was distracted by nail polish; I daintily painted. I liked its bleachy smell and the way it slowly hardened on my blistered skin and shined.

"I just feel so alive when I'm around her. Like I want to stop time and spend seven years in medical school so I can save her life if she happens to get stung and goes into anaphylactic shock." Monica had a bee-sting allergy.

"Sure," I said. "Save her life."

Nathaniel had gotten me the gig. He was savvier than me, pluckier, bigger in the biceps. Had a surfer thing going on. Not bleach blond in a mimbo way, just tan and easy. Same patchy beard all the hip ones had, hints of amber in the chin hairs. Two years below me in film school, but he'd caught up careerwise. His résumé was up on all the job boards. Had a website with built-in Flash and a slick montage. I was shitty at self-promoting. Sent my thesis screenplay around in manila envelopes awaiting return.

"I should probably get an EpiPen and carry it on me. Just in case."

"I thought Felix would be here by now."

We knew Felix was coming, but we didn't know when. He'd written the script and was associate producer. He'd been nominated for an Academy Award. Some people said Felix was a genius. We (the L.A. people) had read the new script. It was good, better than good. Better than the other crap we worked on: thirty-second spots for regional fast-food chains, student shorts, overfunded indie twee. Nathaniel had even done a blockbuster, some sci-fi thing in Death Valley, CGI spaceships crop-dusting the desert. It was a fact Nathaniel never let me forget. He said craft service served Kobe beef and goat-cheese sliders. The food might have been good, but the movie certainly wasn't.

Felix's script was different: sexy, savage, utterly bleak. In short: Art. We imagined being thanked in the acceptance speech ("I'd just like to thank the wonderful crew, whose hard work really made this movie come to life"). We imagined our résumés, our next jobs, moving up in the industry, moving out of our tiny apartments, buying new cars, using those cars to convince women to have sex with us.

We wanted a movie that might one day be called a "film," that we could refer to at a dinner party ten years down the line, light a cigarette and say, "We were naive kids. We thought we were taking the world by storm."

There were problems. The director and the star hated each other; everyone hated the first AD; the first AD was a cokehead and running out of coke; the star had fucked the costar, then her assistant; the production was out of money; the DP had also fucked her assistant; the dailies looked amateur; the food was shit; the Texans thought the L.A. folks were homosexuals; the L.A. folks were mostly homosexuals and took umbrage.

By the time Felix showed up, hope was lost. The director, Andrew Solstice, had lost interest. He spent most of his time trying on cowboy hats, posing in the hair/makeup mirrors, and blowing residue from his finger gun.

It was the day we had the rain machine. Solstice wanted it for the scene in the car when Francisco tells Monica he killed her boyfriend. A bad idea—too soap opera for a subtle picture like this one. In my imagining of the film, the sun beats like a tanning-bed light, providing alien glow, almost X-ray vision to their emaciated torsos.

I stood twenty yards away doing lockup. In a city like Los Angeles this generally meant blocking off a major street corner, stopping pedestrians from barging into your shot. Here there were no pedestrians, only sand and weedy fields. It was just past dawn. In the distance was the Corpus Christi coast, pink sky interrupted by oil rigs. Fake rain fell heavy on the picture car, a rusted blue Mustang.

I didn't know what to make of Francisco, the talent. He'd been a child star of the Mexican stage, and later the hunky adulterer on a popular telenovela. His mother was an opera singer, and his father handcrafted violins. Rumor had it his maternal grandfather had made his nut in munitions.

Francisco played seven instruments and was fluent in as many languages. He'd grown up in a fenced-off estate outside Mexico City with verandas, Ferraris, and armed guards—all the gaudy signifiers of cartel superwealth. Still, he played himself off as a man of the people, spoke Spanish with the Mexican grips and electricians, kicked the soccer ball between takes, smiled a humble, punchable smile at everyone he passed. His acting was iffy, but his face was an exemplar of symmetry and composition. My jealousy was undermined by my interest in starfucking. I had hoped to befriend him, swill tequila by the motel pool. I wanted to ask about the queeny Argentine director who'd kicked him off set for being three pounds overweight. But I was rarely close to the cast members. They ate at different hours. Some nights, though, Francisco would sit with his eyes closed on the motel's shared balcony and pluck a nylon-stringed guitar. The insomniacs among us would come out of our rooms, slowly at first, lingering in our doorways and then gradually getting closer until we'd formed an impromptu audience. Francisco would open his eyes, blush, and apologize for waking us. We'd all say nah and urge him on—as he knew we would—and he'd close his eyes again, allowing just the hint of a smile to cross his lips as he moved into another song.

"What is this cockshit?" someone behind me said.

I turned. Felix wore camo pants and a sleeveless tee. Hair long and greasy, facial features exaggerated: comically oversize mouth and nose. Like late-career Bogart: rheumy-eyed, beyond saving.

"It's raining," I said.

"It's fucking Texas," he said, stormed past me, headed for the set, where he grabbed Solstice by his mullet tail, pulled him under the rain machine, threatened to remove his genitals if he didn't remove the rain machine.

I was approached by first AD Mark Tipplehorn.

"You idiot," he said. "You were supposed to be locking up."

"He was like a bull," I said.

"You idiot," he said again, and wiped his forearm across his face.

Tipplehorn's uniform was all white every day: sneakers, socks, shorts, shirt, visor. He was going for "asshole from L.A. stranded in small town." He wore reflective aviators, scratched chigger bumps.

"Towel me," he said.

I pulled his towel from my pocket and tossed it over.

"I've got a new job for you, anyway. I need an ounce of weed as fast as you can get it."

Tipplehorn had worked with Felix before. Felix thought he had say over what happened on set.

"Weed's the only way to calm him down," Tipplehorn explained. "Also someone to give him a haircut; he likes to have his hair cut on location."

The haircut would be easier to get than the weed, but he wanted the weed first so he could be stoned during the haircut. For the weed I had to approach a Texan. The Texans hated us, but some hated us less than others. Luckily, a kind woman bummed a cigarette off me, called me "sweetheart," and agreed to help with both my tasks. Her name was Kathleen, and she was the on-set hairdresser.

Kathleen didn't give a shit about the higher-ups like Tipplehorn. Just did her thing in the hair trailer, smoking bats and talking on speakerphone to her teenage daughter, who was spending the summer at an arts camp outside Denton. When they said good-bye, Kathleen waved her hand as if her daughter could see her from the other end of the line. She said, "Girl," and her daughter said, "Bye now," and Kathleen looked in the mirror and saw me behind her, squint-eyed in the barber's chair, finally sun-shaded, almost asleep.

"Now about that marijuana," she said.

"You got any nail-polish remover?" I said.

We sat on the edge of Felix's bed facing the television, which was playing dailies. Francisco drove across the bridge into sunset.

"You can imagine the lush strings," Felix said, and threw the remote against the wall. Batteries fell to the floor, rolled to opposite corners of the room. I handed him the blunt.

"Straight men smoke blunts," he said. "Instead of sucking big black cocks."

"Oh?"

"That's why you'll never see a fag smoke a blunt. Their cravings are satisfied. They smoke little joints and prance around thinking about all those beautiful pricks shooting cum like shooting stars across the galaxy of their faces."

"Poetic," I said.

"I want to show you something," Felix said, fast-forwarded the tape.

The scene where the dog runs into the road and Francisco doesn't stop the car until Monica screams and grabs the wheel. We'd spent four hours on it because the dog kept running the wrong way.

"This fucking dog—too pretty. Of course he wants to run it over. Who doesn't want to crush that smug bitch? Dog's not even running right. This is supposed to be suicide. We need an ugly dog, some kind of mutt, runt of the litter, nothing to live for. I want him lingering on the shoulder, contemplating, then dashing out. Francisco sees the trajectory of the dog's life, refuses to alter its course. It's an act of mercy. An act of love."

"I could love a dog," I said.

"The thing that worries me isn't the dog," Felix said. "It's not the dog at all. What worries me is that if they fucked up the dog, how are they going to deal with the cat?"

Felix took a deep pull, ashed on the carpet.

"The cat is the whole picture; the way he moves through the house at the end. If they get the cat right, then maybe this thing can work."

He passed me the blunt.

"Promise me something," he said. "Promise me you won't let them fuck up the cat."

"I'll do my best," I said.

"I like this guy," Felix said to the TV.

We sat stoned in the hair trailer after an afternoon of me making and remaking iced coffee for Solstice—"more milk," "less milk," "soy milk"—and Felix yelling at Tipplehorn, and Tipplehorn rubbing his nose and saying, "Felix, baby, listen," and Felix throwing his coffee on the ground and kicking the Styrofoam, and then Tipplehorn making me pick up the kicked Styrofoam. Finally the haircut. I sat next to him, watched Kathleen's breasts bob as she moved the clippers, feet dancing in tiny increments, eighth steps in time with the half notes, Patsy Cline crooning sweet and solemn, something about three cigarettes in an ashtray.

"The thing about the cat," Felix said.

Kathleen ran a hand through his hair, said, "Don't worry your pretty head."

She shaved it all off. Felix was ready for battle. I was off to battle with him. In a moment of camaraderie, I'd shaved my head too. He appointed me his assistant, carrier of his marijuana, lieutenant in our army of three (Kathleen was also a lieutenant).

Monica was in her trailer, not coming out. The chiggers had gotten to her, and it was too hot to work. Her assistant stood by the camera truck, sobbing into her own cleavage. Mascara, mixed with sweat, dripped black down her chest and neck. Francisco was there, stroked her hair, called her "sweet pea."

Solstice knocked on Monica's door, said, "The camera never sees your ankles."

"That's not the problem," Nathaniel whispered. "She doesn't want to work with Francisco anymore, ever since he fucked her assistant."

"How do you know?"

"I fucked Monica last night."

He was grinning big, but must have been joking. If he'd slept with Monica it meant the death of the hierarchy. Not that she gave unattainable vibes. Monica was fairly normal—for an actress, anyway. She had a BA in psych with a minor in French. Bumped Brooklyn indie pop from the speaker dock in her trailer. Liked football, the Food Network, and books by Bret Easton Ellis. Hailed from the Carolinas, still sent handwritten checks to her mom and sister. Seemed shy and overwhelmed by the attention. Chain-smoked Parliaments between takes, flipped glossy mags or checked her cell while Kathleen reset her hair. This was supposed to be Monica's break. Next year she'd be up on billboards, airbrushed, overlooking highway traffic.

"I'll talk to her," Felix said, removed his shirt, tied it around his head like a bandanna.

"Be my guest," Solstice said.

Felix stepped up, knocked softly.

"Baby girl," he said. "It's just me, Felix. Let's just talk for a minute. I just want to chat."

The door opened. Felix entered. The rest of us stood waiting outside the trailer. Tipplehorn looked at me, mouthed the word *coffee*.

When I came back, Felix and Monica were walking arm in arm. Monica laughed, smiled, leaned into Felix.

Here's how I imagine it: Felix sits on the bed. He begins to roll a blunt. "Mind if I smoke?" he says. Monica is crying. Wordless, Felix takes a bottle of clear nail polish from the top of her dresser and applies it to Monica's ankles. "Men are scum," he says. He slowly lifts her dress above her waist. He runs the nail brush over the bumps around her bikini line. He hands her the blunt. Monica stops crying. She looks at Felix. He tells her that her role in this film is important, the most important. He tells her to channel her hatred of Francisco into hatred of his character. He tells her this scene, the scene they are about to shoot, it came to him in a dream after his mother died. In his grief he imagined a girl—Monica's character—sitting in a diner booth, sipping soda, making origami birds with the paper place mats.

The scene came out okay. When I told Tipplehorn that I was now Felix's assistant, Tipplehorn said, "No, you're not." People said, "What's with the haircut?"

The thing about night shoots is they go until morning. Now it was six a.m. We were dumping raspberry Emergen-C into our coffees. Monica had retired to the motel. We were shooting just Francisco now, burying the body. Even with cameras and crew, the place felt desolate: a six-foot hole in soft earth, surrounded by marshland, mosquitoes hovering.

The scene was tough to shoot because the body couldn't breathe while being buried. The body was Phil, another actor. He lay naked and tried to stretch his penis with his hand between takes.

"Got a fluffer around here?" Phil said.

"Dead men have hard-ons," Felix said.

Solstice pretended not to hear. If you want an R rating you can't show an erection. Besides, according to the film's time line the body had been dead for hours. I wasn't sure how long dead men stayed aroused.

"Years," Felix said. "Being dead's like being on permanent Viagra. There's no distractions; all you can think about is pussy."

"I didn't know you could think while dead," I said.

"Thinking's overrated," Felix said. "What's important is feeling."

Felix handed me a pen.

"What I want you to do is take the pen, shove it as hard as you can into my leg."

He rolled up his shorts, exposed his hairy thigh.

"Just stab me with the pen. Maybe it's filled with special ink. Maybe it will inspire me."

"Are you sure?"

"Even better idea," Felix said. "Don't stab me."

"I prefer this idea."

"Stab Francisco instead. Next time he walks by, take that pen and jam it up his ass. Maybe then he'll feel something. Maybe he'll learn to act."

"I doubt it," I said.

"Me too," Felix said.

We finished when the sun came up, rose over the rigs, glistened on the oil-slick sand. The oilers were already out, already sweating. They walked across the beach with their hard hats and paper-bag lunches in hand. Silence in the van back to the motel. Kathleen tried to sleep, cheek pressed against the window. Mike Michaels, the wardrobe guy, puked into a plastic bag on the rocky coastal road. I was alive and awake. All that coffee coursing through me, plus the vitamin C.

"I think we really nailed that burial scene," I said. "Really captured the light and the feeling."

"Shh," Kathleen said.

"Things are looking up," I said. "Now that Felix is here. As long as the cat works out I think it will be okay. I think things are really looking up."

I heard a couple of grunts. Nathaniel told me to shut up. We passed the local bar. I imagined the inside, lit only by a prism of light from the one tiny window.

Back at the motel everything was bright: the awning, the cars in the parking lot, the glare from the turned-off television. Our A/C sputtered and died. I blew dust from the ancient window, willed in a breeze.

"Yo, Nat," I said. "Let's get out of this shithole, find a diner or something. I feel like eggs."

"Sorry, brah," he said. "Other plans."

Nathaniel claimed he was going to Monica's room to have sex with her. I followed him into the hall, watched while he knocked on her door. She opened, stood framed by the doorway, wrapped in a black bathrobe, hair wet, hanging, impossibly clean. She pulled him in.

Felix had to stay up and watch dailies. I imagine him pacing his room, blinds drawn, take after take rolling across the screen, room heavy with blunt smoke. Phone is ringing. It rings and rings. Eventually Felix unplugs the phone and throws it against the wall.

Gil Broome, the on-set animal wrangler, wore the biggest belt buckles I've ever seen. Different buckles every day. He had a bull buckle, a horse buckle, a cowboy-boot buckle, and one with a diamond-studded state of Texas.

Gil had been in Los Angeles for a short while, a city that didn't suit him. Too many cars, not enough horses. Homesick for animals, he offered to walk a neighbor's dog. Each morning he'd take the dog to the dog park among the actresses and their purse poodles. One day he met another walker, a man of about his own age. The man wore floral-print shirts but had a deep, kind voice and knew enough about the racetrack. They walked together each morning. Do you like music? the man asked Gil. Gil replied that he did enjoy music, mostly country like Merle Haggard and of course Johnny Cash. Have you ever heard of Neil Diamond? the man asked. I believe I recognize the name, Gil said, but for the life of me I can't place it. Well, I'm Neil Diamond, the man said. He changed the subject. Do you like drinking, Gil? Yes, sir, I do, Gil said.

He told a story about his Navy SEAL days on the cleanup crew for the space shuttle *Challenger*. He described the debris, the unrecognizable metal, the smell that might have been the smell of space, the intact finger he claimed he'd found and kept for a souvenir.

Gil gave me his card, invited me to visit his ranch in West Texas. We could ride horses across his acres and drink whiskey under the stars. When the film was over I could show up at Gil's ranch, backpack slung over my shoulder. I'd be his apprentice, learn the trade; my skin would darken; we'd cook baked beans over an open fire. A neighbor girl wore cutoff denim skirts, no shoes. Never met a Jew before. Neil Diamond would visit. We'd sit on the porch and sing "Sweet Caroline."

Felix hated Gil from the moment he saw him.

"You," Felix said, "you there with the mustache."

"Yes, sir," Gil said. "Gil Broome, hombre."

"Gil Broome," Felix said. "I want to talk to you, Gil Broome."

Gil was standing, eating eggs off a paper plate. He was on set today because of chickens; Francisco kills a chicken in front of Monica. They didn't really need Gil because the special-effects people were in charge of the fake chicken and its head. Gil was there to judge authenticity and to keep track of the real chickens that wandered through the background.

"No one cares about the dog," Felix said. "I care about the dog, but the dog's not what we're talking about."

Felix placed an arm on Gil's shoulder.

"Fuck the chickens too," he said. "This scene wasn't in the script anyway."

"No chickens," Gil said. "Got it."

"Yes chickens," Felix said. "Just fuck them. You see what I'm saying?"

Gil looked perplexed. He took a bite of his eggs.

Felix pointed at the eggs. "All that chickens are good for."

Gil smiled.

"What we're talking about is the cat," Felix said.

"What cat?"

"What cat? I like this guy. What cat? The cat that walks through the burning house in the final shot. The death cat. The beautiful agony black cat."

"Beautiful agony?"

"Look. You fucked up the dog. Wrong dog, ran the wrong way. I'm over the dog. But it can't happen again. The cat has to be beautiful. Small green eyes. Completely black. It's got to move slowly up the stairs. It's got to look around, smell death. Can you promise me that, Gil, can you promise me the cat will smell death? That when it says in the script, 'Cat walks up the stairs,' the cat will dance through that house like he's Mikhail fucking Baryshnikov?"

Gil put his plate down on a bench, as if, like a cat, he sensed the threat of physical danger.

"Cat can't read your script," Gil said. "Cat can't read."

Felix's face went scarily still. Only his eyes moved. He scanned from Gil's nose to his own clenched fist. Knuckles bubbled and shifted beneath the stretched skin. Felix flexed his biceps; they were tried-and-true weapons for getting his way. I took a step back, but Gil didn't budge, coughed out a laugh.

"You, Gil Broome, you can read my script. That's the thing. That's what we're paying you for. To read the script and then whisper some Doctor Dolittle whatever the fuck into the cat's ear so he'll do what it says in the script."

"Cat's not an actor," Gil said. "Cat doesn't take notes."

"So let me get this straight," Felix said. "Your job title, right, you're a wrangler, an animal wrangler? Am I correct that that is the title of your job, that on the call sheet it says 'Gil Broome, Animal Wrangler'?"

"Yes, sir, that is correct."

"Because as far as I can tell, Gil, Gil Broome, as far as I can tell, you're just a fucking pet owner. You're just a guy with a cat."

"Cat can't read," Gil said.

Tipplehorn approached. He was good at his job; he knew when to break up a conversation. "Gil, you're needed on set."

I was supposed to hold an umbrella over Monica, shield her from the sun. Her assistant had been fired, sent back to L.A. with a half-decent story, waiting for a call from Francisco that never comes. Monica didn't need me, but there was protocol. Her skin was gold from an adolescence spent sitting shotgun in drop-tops, joyriding the Outer Banks. Now she was someone and sat in my shade. A website had spotted her finger-picking from the salad bar at Whole Foods in West Hollywood. A true coronation.

"I'm sorry you have to do this," Monica said. "I know it's incredibly degrading."

"That's nice of you to say," I said, but she was already back to ignoring my existence. Stared at the script pages, her highlighted lines. I could hear her mumbling. My arm ached. It had only been a minute.

"I could practice with you if you want?" I said.

Monica turned, assessed. I could see my reflection in her oversize shades: peeling nose and stubbly dome, the glop of excess sunscreen on my chin.

"Sure," she said. "I guess. You do Francisco."

I read, "Baby don't, baby don't cry, c'mon."

She read, "Oh, fuck off."

"Baby don't . . . ," I read, and leaned in as the stage directions said. Smelled lavender, honey blossom, a thin strain of uterine blood. My nose against her neck fuzz. My shallow breathing.

"What the fuck are you doing?" Monica said.

"Acting?"

"Jesus Christ," she said, stood, sauntered off, left me holding the umbrella over nothing.

That night, the storm. One of those passing tropical numbers. Black clouds like Mexican chimney smoke rising up the

Gulf, covering the coastline. They get one every summer. Felix didn't want to shoot in the rain for the same reason that Solstice did—melodrama. Tipplehorn had a more convincing argument—money—and he won. Felix was angry and took it out on the wardrobe guy, who didn't have shoes the right color for Little Brother. Little Brother was in sneakers, was supposed to be in dress shoes, church shoes. Felix tried to color the white sneakers with black marker. Because everything was wet, the marker wouldn't adhere. Felix threw the sneakers in the mud. I had to retrieve the sneakers, give them back to the kid who now had to wear wet shoes.

According to Nathaniel, Tipplehorn had run out of cocaine. "I want him off my set," he said, referring to Felix. He told me to get the DV cam from the camera truck. "Tell Felix, he told me, that you're shooting a behind-the-scenes documentary. Take him under the craft-service tent and interview him for as long as he'll let you."

I didn't like deceiving Felix but told myself they might actually use the footage when they saw how Felix opened up to me.

We marched to the craft-service tent, a culinary oasis where Darrell the craft-service chef presided over the cast's unreasonable requests: Vermont maple syrup, organic soy milk, fair-trade Colombian coffee, and other things you couldn't get in Corpus.

I struggled with my tripod, which was sinking in the mud. The truck drivers laughed at me from their own tent. They were Texan and in the Teamsters union. Got paid time and a half when it rained. Plus overtime. I couldn't steady the camera on the sinking tripod, so I just said fuck it and went handheld.

Felix said, "Do you have an agent? You don't have an agent, why would you have an agent? I have an agent, and I have a manager, and my agent has an assistant, and my manager has an assistant, and right at this moment they're poring over scripts asking, Is this the next Felix? Is that the next Felix? Because Felix is done and we've got money to spend, all this fucking money, and we need an army of Felixes marching the streets of Los Angeles with their Final Draft printouts, their Terrence Malick–inspired voice-overs, their hunger."

I'd managed to focus but was having trouble getting him in frame. He moved, paced, grabbed handfuls of candy corn and stuffed his face.

"And all these assistants have meetings," he said, still chewing. "And they meet with the higher-ups, like my agent and manager, and they all wear shirts unbuttoned at the collar, like one fucking button too many, just so they can say I have hair on my chest, I do not have breasts, in this shell of a body there is something animal that still exists, that is ruthless, that will ruin other men and supply my office with a mini fridge and excellent air-conditioning. I'm not allowed in the meetings, but I know what goes on: they sit around, and he's Geppetto. You remember Geppetto?"

The rain came now in sulfuric sheets. Others arrived around us, edged in on our shelter, chomped cheese balls, tortilla chips. Nathaniel had taken over umbrella duty. He escorted Monica to her trailer. Her nipples were visible through her soaked summer dress. Big nipples that took up most of her little breasts. Nathaniel had a hand on the small of her back, but she was a step ahead, almost running. When Nathaniel tried to follow her into the trailer, Monica gave a small shove and said something I couldn't hear. She shut the door. Nathaniel stood shocked for a moment. The soundtrack in his head played maudlin classical. The camera caught a tear coming down his cheek. The audience empathized. Nathaniel looked out at the horizon before remembering real life and that he was soaking and still on the clock.

My camera kept rolling. Others talked, drowned him out. Tipplehorn, in rain goggles and white Gore-Tex shell, saying, "What I'd give right now for a soy chai latte."

Felix didn't notice. He said, "I'm this little fucking doll, and I'm surrounded by Geppettos, and each one has a different string and they're pulling my strings, my limbs are flopping everywhere, and they're saying who's going to direct? What kind of box office? Maybe if we change the ending?"

Nathaniel sidled up to me, clearly still in disbelief. But he was playing it cool. He said, "I'm thinking this thing with Monica wasn't such a good idea. Actresses . . ."

I shushed him, nodded at Felix.

Nathaniel said, "You wanna get out of here? They're calling the shoot anyway. Equipment's too wet. Let's ditch this and find a couple beers. We can hide out in the hair trailer while they pack."

"I'm busy," I said.

The cat wouldn't go up the stairs. One of the grips had to rush home and get his cat, a gray cat, not even the right color. I put a tin of sardines at the top of the staircase and the grip's cat got it right. The scene was completed. Solstice said that's a wrap, and we took cold beers out of picnic coolers and patted each other on the back. We returned to the motel, watched the sun lazily emerge. Day after the rain and everything smelled like wet oil and ragweed. Francisco had his guitar out by the pool, and Kathleen did her best Loretta Lynn.

When it went to DVD, Nathaniel and I were in Brooklyn, sharing the ground floor of a freestanding Victorian in Ditmas Park. We had hardwood floors and original molding, and we got a grand feeling eating cereal under our twelve-arm chandelier. New York was nice; everything was expensive, but you didn't need money. You could take a girl to the nearest dive, drink cheap pitchers, and tell her about your brush with Francisco Gomez, the way he closed his eyes when he played guitar. The girl would grab your wrist. Then you'd lean in close to talk over the DJ, say something like, "I've got a record player and some beers back at my place," and let her ride sidesaddle on your single-speed bike through the falling snow.

We were finding work, or Nathaniel was anyway. I liked the cold nights, smoking out my cracked window, staring at the empty yellow cabs that lined our block. Off-duty drivers speaking loudly on cell phones in Cantonese and Arabic and Staten Island English.

People came over for the screening—Nathaniel's idea. Put out cheese and hummus, a jug of Rossi. Crowded onto the couch. Nathaniel was wearing a cowboy hat. The girls appreciated irony; they'd gone to art school. Gwen, Nathaniel's latest thing, had stringy hair, a shrill laugh, and fingers pink at the joints from New York winter. She wrote for a weekly paper that published blind items about people we knew, or at least that we were friends with on Facebook. Nathaniel had his arm around her. Gwen's friend Anne sat to Nathaniel's left, her fishnetted legs up on the coffee table. She said the phrase *shit, man* at all possible instances—when she saw the chandelier, when she saw the TV, when she saw Nathaniel's Texas-flag tattoo.

Two girls I didn't know sat cross-legged on the floor. One was beautiful but kept checking her cell phone, awaiting better plans. The other had eaten Adderall and blew gum bubbles she then poked with a mechanical pencil. "Roll tape," she said, then said it again. "Action," she said, and Nathaniel dimmed the lights.

Title screen, then open on an empty beach, littered with foil and aluminum, cigarette cellophane blowing in the wind. Pan across to the oil rigs. Long-muscled men, like evolved primates, hang from the machinery's rungs. And there I am in my brief appearance as an extra. They'd needed people to swell out the crowd. I look ridiculous as a roughneck, draped in too-large Carhartt, hard hat in hand. The camera only sees me for a second. I'm sweating and blotchy, and my shaved head has a bull's-eye sunburn.

Everyone laughed, and I felt myself blush.

"You look like a dork," Gwen said. Nathaniel agreed. The other blew a confirmative bubble. But Anne looked over, gave a nod of recognition, said, "Shit, man."

It was all wrong. What I wanted was the action just offscreen. I wanted Tipplehorn screaming indecipherable instructions across all walkie frequencies; Solstice silly in boots and unnecessary spurs; Kathleen on speakerphone in the hair trailer, oblivious to outside commotion; Nathaniel hidden behind a garbage can, whispering "Cut" to a featured extra.

I looked at Nathaniel when Monica made her debut. They'd given her entrance music, some too-obvious C & W ballad about lost innocence. Monica stands on the porch, watches Francisco watch her from his parked Mustang. Nathaniel's face didn't move, but I saw him ball a fist around a skinny hipster hand.

Then the house is on fire, flames reaching up into Texas night. They'd gotten the colors right, a hundred shades of orange, gray, and blue. We were coming to the cat's coda, the feline waltz that Felix had dreamed about. I hoped Solstice hadn't screwed it up in editing. I wanted Felix to have that victory. Anne got up, stretched, shook her curly hair from its bun, and bent to tie a shoelace. She walked toward the kitchen, asked if I wanted another beer. The cat did its thing, but I wasn't watching. I was in another movie, myself the star, Anne lit by the headlights of a passing cab.

THE PORCHIES

It started with Grace. Jason was heading back to Philly for the summer to work at his father's carpet-cleaning company. None of us knew why. Maybe carpet cleaning runs in the blood. My theory was he had some action back there he didn't want us to know about for fear we'd tell his girlfriend. It was good thinking on his part. We weren't malicious people, but considering the amount of alcohol we consumed on a weekly basis, someone was bound to let it slip.

Whatever the reason, Jason was gone, and we needed a subletter. Or rather, he needed a subletter. The rest of us didn't care if the room stayed empty and Jason had to pay his share of the rent while he wasn't even there. This option, however, defeated the purpose of Jason's plan to live rent-free with his parents. Jason was determined to find someone, and we were determined that whoever he found not be a complete and total loser. So really it became a group project.

There were two major obstacles. First and foremost was the house. It wasn't entirely our fault. The house had been falling apart long before we'd leased it. Our landlord was a big man named Big Frank. The upkeep of our duplex was not his main concern. Once the front door fell off and it took him a week to put it back on.

Neither (and this is why we got the house) was he concerned with the fact that we crammed seven people into a house zoned for four by stashing beds in tiny, windowless rooms in the basement. This is an exaggeration. Only one room was windowless. Jason's. Though to call it a room would be unfair. It was a closet, and no one in his right mind would live there by choice. That is, no one except for Jason, who liked that it stayed dark enough to sleep all day.

The other obstacle was ourselves. No one had done the dishes in weeks, and the kitchen was infested with flies. The power had gone out recently because we'd forgotten to pay the bill. The food in the fridge went bad and stank. Eventually someone, I think it was Donny, couldn't take it anymore and mailed the check. The power came back on, and we sort of cleaned the fridge. By sort of, I mean we tossed all the meat except one pack of hot dogs Mike F. claimed wouldn't go bad.

Although the kitchen was the worst room, it barely took the gold over the living room, with my room, perhaps, coming a close third. But you get the idea. The details aren't important. This isn't a story about the house, or even us, but one about the Porchies. And, as I said, it started with Grace.

Here's what happened: no one wanted the room. I couldn't blame them. Jason, sensing failure, and being the crafty guy that he was, put an ad for the room online—on some kind of Boston message board. This was pre-Craigslist; Jason was ahead of his time. His assumption being that someone in another state might be moving to Boston, desperate for any room, see the cheap price, and blindly hop on board. Because this person would be out of state, he or she wouldn't have a chance to look at the room before entering into a contract. A week later, a small Asian girl unpacked a blue Ford with Florida plates.

Grace accepted her windowless fate with no hint of emotion. She moved in quietly. Not once did she complain about the smells or the stickiness of the floor. In fact, unless you were paying attention (I was), you might not have noticed her at all amid the trash, the clutter, and the revolving cast of guests and girlfriends who breezed in and out of our door each day, stepping lightly to avoid sleeping people on the floor as if they were land mines. Someone once overheard the neighbors say, "They live like Mexicans in there." We recited the story with pride. It was better to be Mexicans than middle-class college kids.

Aside from the seven rent payers we had three "extended stay" guests. These were people who'd shown up one day and never left. The first and longest-standing of these guests was Tommy C-Slice. C-Slice was a friend who'd taken time off from school to go back to Queens and sell dime bags off his bicycle. He was a funny guy, half-Dominican, with skinny dreads and a penchant for dry sarcasm. After some coaxing, we convinced C-Slice to come for a visit, unaware that he would never leave.

C-Slice was not obtrusive upon our lifestyle. He watched TV all day and hand-rolled cigarettes. He had no income and survived on scraps of people's leftovers. We liked him.

We also had the Junkie Sisters. The Junkie Sisters were younger, dropouts. They slept with my housemates in (un-written) exchange for room and board. No one minded them either, mostly because they were good-looking and walked around in short shorts. They both chain-smoked and were always high. I don't think either of them ate food. It was C-Slice who coined the nickname.

What I'm getting at is that we were a happy family before Grace came along, and that Grace was small and it was easy for her to disappear into the windowless room in the basement, out of sight and beyond the general concern of the roommates.

I tried to help Grace move in. I carried things from the car, offered to go to Target. She was unreceptive, though not unfriendly.

Grace was plain-looking too. Her skin was terrible: dry, acne-scarred. Some guys don't mind that, but it's one of my turnoffs. I like soft skin. The point is that my inter-est in Grace wasn't sexual. I was convinced of my love for Annie, who'd blown me to Jimi Hendrix's "Star-Spangled Banner" before heading home to California for the sum-mer. I entertained fantasies of driving cross-country and showing up at her doorstep, but I knew that I wouldn't, and that even if I did she wouldn't want me around.

Instead, I spent my time writing awful love letters that went unanswered. She thought they were creepy, but I didn't know that and still clung to the belief that my surfer girl would return, tanned, into my arms, come September.

It was probably because of my ongoing infatuation with Annie that I turned my attention to Grace instead of a romantic prospect. That Grace didn't want to have anything to do with the rest of us didn't bother me. I was happy to watch her life from the wings. It gave me something to do.

I didn't have a job that summer because my father had died a few months earlier and left me some money. It hadn't been a pleasant year. Like Grace, I'd spent a lot of time indoors. I watched reality TV, particularly *Survivor*. I was engrossed in the race for survival: the backstabbing and manipulation—the strategy, will, temerity, and luck that it took to survive. I lost touch with my friends. I passed my classes because of grade inflation and because some of my teachers knew about my dad and felt bad for me.

I met Annie at a frat party. I don't remember what I said to her or she to me, but we kissed. I thought she was beautiful. I told her she was beautiful. She'd gone to an all-girls Catholic school and wore a tiny silver cross around her neck, though she claimed to be an atheist and hate her parents. For me, a Jewish boy with a dead father, there was something deeply alluring about the way she wore that cross, secretly, beneath the clothes she now let me remove. Or maybe it just reminded me of a Billy Joel song. When she slept I fingered the cross and whispered, "I love you," just to see how the words sounded coming out of my mouth.

This was a week before school ended. We spent the week drinking wine, making out, eating takeout. I thought we were soul mates. I don't think Annie agreed. I drove her to the airport on a Saturday morning. We kissed in the car for the last time.

Once school ended and she was gone, I went back to my lethargy. I didn't want to get a job and didn't plan to. The problem was, I wasn't sure what else to do. I figured Donny and I could go fishing on weekends and I'd watch reruns during the day. Maybe get some reading done. At night I'd drink and sit outside with no shirt on. I was bored within a week, but there was no turning back.

Summer in Boston is slow and humid. The students leave and the heat smothers you. If you don't have A/C, you're fucked. We didn't. We had an intricately designed system of fans that only worked if you were standing directly in front of one. I paced from fan to fan and thought about Annie. It was too hot to sleep. I'd get up early, smoke cigarettes on the porch with C-Slice. We'd watch our neighbors leave for work. They would get in their cars, sweating in their dress shirts, tightening their ties. They looked at us and I knew they hated us. Sometimes we'd drink Bud Light or Bloody Marys, but usually it was too hot for drinking. We didn't talk much, which was okay with me.

The Junkie Sisters never came out on the porch. They hogged the TV and watched girl crap too—Home and Garden—indulging some secretly harbored domestic fantasy. Usually they'd fall asleep in front of the TV and I'd come in and steal the remote. They were often up all night doing coke and ecstasy. By the time it cooled down in the afternoon they tended to pass out. The rest of the house went to work during the day. Except for Grace. She stayed in her room and talked on her cell phone to her boyfriend. I sometimes listened to their conversations through the vent. Grace's voice was quiet, and I couldn't hear much, but there seemed something tender in her tone, something warm. Soon I would meet her boyfriend and the rest of the Porchies.

In the meantime I did more of the same and nothing happened. My mother called me crying several times, insisting that I come home for summer and spend time with her and my brother. I stopped answering her calls when I saw her name on the ID.

Donny and I went to his parents' cabin in the Berkshires during the last weekend of June to go fishing. We had wanted to go before, but he was working in a lab and kept getting stuck there on Saturdays. No one else came. Dan and Jay spent their weekends having sex with the Junkie Sisters; Mike C. went to visit his girlfriend in Connecticut; Mike F. sold hot dogs at Fenway; C-Slice never went anywhere. "Keeping an eye on the house," he'd say.

This isn't one of those stories where going fishing reminds me of my dead father and I get maudlin. He wasn't an outdoor guy; he was more into watching sports on TV. I learned to fish at summer camp when I was twelve. If anything, fishing made me nostalgic for girls wrapped in towels wearing their bikini tops in the dining hall to show off for older boys.

We didn't catch much. I liked drinking beer with Donny and shooting the shit, grilling hot dogs.

"What do you think of Grace," I asked him.

"Who's Grace?" he said.

It was understandable. Donny worked a lot.

During the day we swam in the lake and played one-on-one Wiffle ball. It felt good to move my body again after all that time on the couch. I liked the way the wind felt when I took my shirt off.

The drive home was peaceful. I slept and Donny drove. I'd wake up and catch glimpses of the mountains, hear snatches of oldies coming from the radio, then fall back asleep.

When we got back it was drizzling. Three guys sat on the covered porch drinking Budweiser and eating pizza. I was still half asleep and wasn't alarmed.

"Hey," I said. I lit a cigarette.

"What's crappening?" one of the guys responded. He was funny-looking, with a fifties-style flattop and a big, round belly. He looked about our age.

"Who are you?" Donny said. He was tired from driving and slightly on edge.

"Chill," the dude said. "I'm Jeff, Grace's boyfriend."

"Oh," I said. "I'm Seth."

"I'm Donny," Donny said. "We live here."

Jeff's friends introduced themselves. They had thick Boston accents, no Rs. Probably townies.

Donny and I went inside. The dudes stayed on the porch for another couple hours, drinking. Eventually the two guys who weren't Grace's boyfriend left. Jeff came in and went down to Grace's room. He gave a nod as he walked past.

"Gonna get laid," he said, and smiled.

When he was gone, I asked C-Slice, "What's the word on that guy?"

"Townie," C-Slice said.

"He asked me what's crappening," I said.

"Bizarre," C-Slice replied.

It was still raining when I woke up. Jeff was gone. I watched TV with the Junkie Sisters, drank coffee. C-Slice slept on the couch. The rain made it feel like a Sunday, and maybe it was one.

By five thirty the sun was out and Jeff and his buddies were back on the porch drinking Budweiser and eating pizza. I didn't say anything. No one did. They came back the next day too and the next and the next. Five thirty each day, and they were gone by nine, ten if there was a Sox game. They listened to the games on a portable radio. On the fourth day I invited them in to watch the game with the rest of us.

"No," Jeff said. "We'd just stink up the joint." He talked like he was in a greaser movie.

"Okay," I said, and went back inside.

"What's the deal with those dudes?" I said to C-Slice.

"Porchies, dude," he said, "just Porchies."

The Porchies became commonplace. Aside from C-Slice and me, the housemates were too busy to pay attention. I watched them through the window. I liked looking at Jeff. He was an animated speaker, constantly waving his arms, moving his body. The fat around his cheeks gave his face a cartoon look.

The other Porchies weren't as interesting. Al was short and blond with wavy hair and big arms. Steve was scrawny. He wore wifebeaters and had eagle wings tattooed between his shoulders.

I made a habit of inviting them in, but they never accepted. Every day when his friends left, Jeff would walk past us on the way to Grace's room and say something about the fact that he was about to have sex. It was different each time, and it became a part of the day I anticipated. Once he said, "It's fornicatin' time," and the next day, "Get ready for the horizontal tango."

"That's disgusting," one of the Junkie Sisters would remark.

July Fourth came shortly after the Porchies' arrival. We decided to have a party. My brother was coming to town for the weekend, and I wanted to show him a good time. I figured his summer had to be pretty shitty dealing with Mom. He deserved to let loose.

Derek showed up an hour before the party started. He looked worn out. He was still in high school, and it must have been a lot to handle. We sat on the porch drinking and smoking until the guests arrived. We talked about Boston bands and how there was nothing good on TV in summer. I asked him if he'd been to any Sox games this year. He hadn't. We couldn't talk about the big stuff, but that was okay. It was good just sitting together.

Parties in summer are a whole different scene, a melting pot of stragglers: townies, people's high school friends, neighbors—whoever's around. It's easy to get laid because things that happen in summer don't feel like part of real life. Still, I didn't want to try, though I'd given up on Annie. She hadn't responded to my letters, and I knew it was because they were weird.

I hardly recognized anyone at the party. Mike F.'s Fenway friends were there, and Mike C.'s girlfriend had shown with some girls from her hometown. There were frat dudes and hippies. Everyone got along fine. We had two kegs of cheap beer and a lot of marijuana.

At some point the Porchies showed up. They weren't usually around on weekends. I had invited them but assumed they wouldn't come. They took their spot on the porch. They didn't have pizza this time.

The Porchies had a lot of company. The porch is a popular spot in summer, especially during parties. People like to smoke outside and mingle. I watched from the window as drunk people talked to Jeff. Jeff made the drunks laugh easily.

I didn't spend the whole time watching the Porchies. I'm not a stalker or anything. I walked around, mostly to and from the keg. I talked baseball with Mike F.'s Fenway friends and said hello to people I hadn't seen in a while. Mike C.'s girlfriend introduced me to her home friends. They were cute and younger, and I thought I could hook up with one if I wanted. But I didn't have it in me, and I remember feeling like I'd never have it in me again.

When I went back to the window, Grace was out there, sitting on Jeff's lap. She held a beer and looked up at the streetlamp as if it were a full moon. Her mouth was curved slightly upward in a soft smile. It was a secretive smile, almost embarrassed, but clearly there as she fixed on the artificial light and Jeff bounced her on his knee, blowing smoke rings.

I felt an arm around my shoulder and immediately knew it was my brother. It was strange to feel another person's skin against my own, his red cheeks inches from my face. It was the first physical contact I'd had with another human being in a long time.

"Who is that guy?" Derek asked me.

"Jeff Porch," I said.

"Pretty weird, " he said. "He told me he was gonna shove a tube of toothpaste up my ass."

"Sounds about right," I said. "I think he's a good guy though."

"Tell that to your neighbor," Derek said.

"What?"

"Jeff Porch called him a douche and then said he fucked his daughter with a corn on the cob."

"Shit," I said.

I looked at Jeff. He was smiling.

The party wound down. People left, drifting out the door, lingering in the doorway to say good-bye, or else disappearing hand in hand to a patch of grass outside because it was still warm and the neighborhood was quiet. I didn't notice when the Porchies left, just that they were gone. My roommates were gone too, and I guessed that most of them were getting laid.

Derek had passed out on the couch. Even in sleep he didn't look peaceful. His breath was heavy, and his legs kept kicking, trying to bend into comfort on the too-small couch. I grabbed one of the blankets that C-Slice usually used, a worn-out red one with a Coca-Cola logo sewn into the stitching. I placed it on my brother with light hands, knowing I wouldn't wake him but trying to be considerate anyway.

When I got down to the basement the music from Grace's room was really loud. Her door was cracked open.

Their bodies were obscured. All I could see was Grace's head from the side, tilted back over the edge of the bed. She was making the same face that I saw her make on the porch, only this time her eyes were closed and her lips were slightly parted to reveal a front tooth biting hard on her bottom lip. A thin trail of blood dripped from her lip, over her chin, and down the nape of her neck.

I avoided the Porchies for a while after July Fourth. When they were on the porch I'd hide in my room listening to CDs. I wanted to write, but I'd given up on writing to Annie and didn't know what else to say.

July moved slowly. Donny was busy with work and couldn't go fishing. I had trouble keeping track of the rest. C-Slice was still around, and we hung out a lot, staring into the television in the hope it would bring us with it to the land of palm trees and police drama. I liked C-Slice because he never asked about my problems and didn't expect to be asked about his. He was unhappy in a way I understood. I don't know what spawned it in him, but it's a certain type of sadness that paralyzes you in front of the television or the fan, chains you to the house.

The Junkie Sisters were the same, and the more I began to realize that, the more I despised them for it—despised them for the fact that they were human beings beneath the shell of intoxication and indifference. To me, they didn't even have names.

They did have names, of course. Louise (Lulu) Dupont and Sarah Grossman. They were both blond. Lulu was from Louisiana and of Cajun origin. Sarah was a Jewish girl from North Jersey. I assumed they both came from money because neither of them worked but they could always afford drugs. They were attractive enough—skinny and pale. But they had those vacant eyes that scared me. I was certain my eyes were the same.

Toward the end of the month, Lulu's mother came. C-Slice and I were on the porch when someone pulled up in a shiny Ford Focus. It must have been a rental. A tall woman appeared. Her blond hair was stringy and pulled back. Mrs. Dupont looked just like Lulu. She stood up straight, marched to our door.

"I'm looking for Louise," she said calmly. "I was told I might find her here."

"Lulu's inside," C-Slice said.

Mrs. Dupont looked through the window. Lulu was sitting on the couch with a cigarette between her fingers. For a second I thought Mrs. Dupont might cry at the sight of her daughter through the window, but she fixed herself, pulled her shoulders back, and remained stoic as she walked through the door to do what she'd come to do.

"How'd you find me?"

"I called your roommate. She said you were probably here."

"I'm not going with you."

Mrs. Dupont stood in front of the TV. I could see Sarah attempting to peer around her at the screen. Lulu put out her cigarette.

"You can't stay here forever," Mrs. Dupont said.

It seemed to apply to all of us. She was looking around, noticing the broken windows, fast-food wrappers, discarded beer cans. They were things I hadn't thought about in a while. Mrs. Dupont leaned over and turned off the TV. You could hear the fans humming.

"C'mon, Louise," she said. She grabbed her daughter's hand and pulled her limp body from the couch.

"Get your things," Mrs. Dupont said. "We'll have to fumigate them."

Lulu tossed a few scraps of clothing in a backpack. As they were walking out she said to me, "Tell Jay good-bye."

I never did. He never asked about it either.

Once Lulu was gone, Sarah didn't last long. I saw it coming. She hardly watched TV anymore. She started putting on makeup and getting out of the house during the day. One day she never came back. No one was sure when, but I'd say it was the last week of July.

She probably found another guy, maybe a houseful of guys like us. Another place where she could watch television and put powder up her nose without the guilt of seeing sad mothers come to rescue their daughters, and without the sadness of not being rescued herself. We weren't special. Boston is a young person's town and was littered with houses exactly like ours. If she was smart, she found a cleaner one.

C-Slice was the next to go. I sensed he was incomplete without the Junkie Sisters. He rarely spoke to them and didn't seem to like them all that much, but they were his in a way that no one else could touch. Lulu and Sarah had shared Dan and Jay's beds at night, but their souls were on the couch, and the couch was C-Slice's territory.

He gave more warning than the others. It was a couple days after we noted the permanent disappearance of Sarah. We were all sitting on the porch drinking. It was the first time the whole gang had hung out together in a while. The Porchies had already left, but even Grace was there, nursing a beer in the corner. It was one of those nights in August when you can still go shirtless at midnight. We all did except for Grace. I noticed how pale my own body looked compared to my roommates' tanned skin. Donny sat on the steps lighting candles, dripping wax onto his forearm. Mike F. tossed a baseball up and down.

"Think it might be getting time to head on out of here," C-Slice said.

"Is that what you reckon?" Donny replied.

I wanted to tell him to stay, but that's not the kind of guy I am, and it wouldn't have mattered anyway.

C-Slice stuck around for a couple more days. He and I watched the street in the mornings like we used to. On Wednesday he walked to the T and was gone.

"Take care of yourself," I told him.

"No doubt, bro," he said.

We stayed friends. I didn't see him much, but if I was ever in New York we'd have drinks and talk about who we'd seen. One of us would always bring up the Porchies.

"Remember Jeff Porch?" C-Slice would say.

"Yeah," I'd reply. "He asked me what's crappening."

We'd laugh for a bit and mutter, "Jeff Porch, dude. Fucking Jeff Porch."

After C-Slice left I was bored and started to watch the Porchies again through the window. One day I even joined them on the porch, bringing out an extra chair from the kitchen. They didn't seem to mind my presence, but I didn't feel included either. I didn't join in when they recited (as they did every day) the inscription on the Budweiser can: "This is the famous Budweiser beer. We know of no brand produced by any other brewer which costs so much to brew and age. Our exclusive Beechwood Aging produces a taste, a smoothness and a drinkability you will find in no other beer at any price." But I did listen to the Sox games on their radio and make comments, and I did sit and drink with them.

I was surprised at how little they talked. For some reason I'd imagined their conversations to be interesting. In actuality they were at least as boring as my own discussions with my roommates. Jeff talked a lot, but he didn't have much to say. Mostly he swore and made sodomy threats. Steve hardly said a word. Al, I learned, was a communist. He worked in a Coca-Cola factory and was big into unions and conspiracy theories. You would think this would spark some good discussion, but in truth, his rhetoric was no different from that of the kids in my sociology classes who I'd grown to hate for their self-righteousness. I guess Al was more deserving of his beliefs; he was, after all, an actual member of the proletariat. But I still found him boring.

"I'll Castro your dick off," Jeff would say. He had a habit of repeating jokes.

Jeff would still make his pre-sex announcement before heading down to Grace's room, but it was awkward because I was the only one he was talking to. I could sense that he felt superior to me in a way, because he was having sex and I wasn't.

One day Jeff was the only Porchie to show up. It was the second week of August, and I wasn't feeling ready for the upcoming school year and the return of life to the city and campus. He was sitting on the porch by himself doing an Axl Rose impression and trying to light a match on his belt buckle.

"Hey, Jeff," I said.

He continued singing, *"Take me down to the Paradise City where the grass is green and the girls are pretty,"* playing air guitar for my benefit.

"Jeff," I said, "how come Grace never hangs out on the porch?"

"Honestly," he said, "she's just shy. I don't make her stay in the basement or anything. She's just not that into partying like me."

"I see," I said.

"I'm gonna head down there. I guess you know what I'm gonna do."

The next day there was a knock on the door. Big Frank stood with his arms crossed. He handed me a piece of paper.

"I have to evict you guys," he said. "Jimmy from next door's been complaining. Said someone's been harassing his daughter, threatening her. Been going on for a while now. Jimmy's an old pal of mine, and he said if it doesn't stop, he'll call the cops. I don't have time to figure out which one of you fuckheads is causing this problem, and I don't care either. I can't have any cops coming here. You knew that when you moved in. I expect you'll all be out by the end of the week."

I was the last one to pack up and leave. Dan and Jay had moved all their stuff to some other friend's house and were staying there until they found a new place. Mike C. said peace out and went to stay with his girlfriend for the rest of the summer, which is where he'd wanted to be the whole time anyway; now he had an excuse to go. Mike F. was from Acton, just a quick drive down Route 2. Donny left in the morning while I was sleeping. He had work at the lab.

No one said good-bye. Everyone knew they'd see each other when school started.

I helped Grace load up her car just as I'd helped unload it at the beginning of the summer. She didn't have much stuff.

"Where you heading?" I asked her. I assumed she was going to Jeff's.

"Florida," she said.

"What about Jeff?"

"Don't think I'm really invited. Besides, these things end sometimes."

She didn't seem sad.

"I guess," I said.

I looked at the house. It wasn't really empty. We'd decided to leave the furniture because it was shitty and falling apart and no one had a car big enough to take it. There was trash everywhere, a sort of fuck-you to Big Frank—literally. Dan and Jay had spelled out "Fuck you" in beer cans on the living room floor.

I didn't have much to take. Mostly clothes, CDs, and the TV from the living room. I carried the TV out to my car and then up to my room in the house I grew up in, which I began referring to as "my mother's house." I watched a lot of TV when I got home, for hours, days, weeks. My brother and I would drink beer on the porch sometimes.

I hardly saw my mother. She stayed in bed most of the time, and when she got up her nightgown would be slipping off one shoulder and her hair would be all crazy and her eyes were barely open. I didn't want to look.

"I'm glad you're here," she said a couple times, which was strange because it didn't even seem as if she'd noticed I was there, but she put her hand on my forehead and ran her fingers through my hair, and I knew she was being honest.

I stole her pills. I thought they might help me relax, which they did. They gave me a numbness that stopped the feeling I had when I paced the halls listening to loud music. It was a feeling like I wanted to smash windows and run screaming down the highway. With the pills I could sleep and I lost my appetite, which was good, because no one ever cooked.

I didn't go back to school in the fall. I couldn't get it together. The others got a new house near the old one. I went over a couple times at the beginning of the semester. There were friends I didn't know, girls. I thought people were looking at me funny, like they thought I'd gone crazy. It was probably nonsense. We'd had a lot of friends on hiatus from school before. I don't know why I thought I was special.

I'm not going to get sentimental and say it was "the summer that changed my life" or anything like that. It wasn't. I've had worse summers since, and certainly more fucked-up ones. The next summer I was in McLean Hospital. I could tell a story about that, about all the crazy people I met there.

After rehab I went back on pills then back in rehab then

drinking then sober. I've had jobs since then that I've quit and ones I've been fired from. I have a job now like the ones my neighbors had when I watched them sweat in their cars, and when I look at myself in the mirror it's with the same hate they looked at me with then.

I've had relationships too, good and bad. I was married for a while. It didn't work out.

My brother got married too. I was the best man but got drunk and punched a waiter in the face for reasons I still don't understand but were supposedly related to a short-age of franks-'n'-blankets.

I watched his marriage dissolve more quickly than my own, though I don't know why it did, because I know Derek was capable of so much love, far more than me, and I was jealous of that and then sad because it didn't matter in the end.

Our mother died at sixty-five of cancer. At the funeral Derek and I stood over her stone, and as the rabbi was talking Derek said, "She's happier down there," and in-stead of feeling trite it felt true.

I saw Jeff Porch one more time. It was the end of fall and the wind was blowing in New England fashion, which is a euphemism for unbearable. I'd been at school signing the necessary papers for my semester off. I was walking back to the T and trying to light a cigarette but failing be-cause of the wind. Not giving up, I stood there repeatedly flicking the lighter until my finger burned with cold and friction. Someone came up behind me.

"Twat's up?" Jeff said.

I gave up on the cigarette, put the lighter away.

"I'm heading home," I said. "What are you up to these days?"

"Going to California," Jeff said, "San Diego, California."

"Sounds warmer than here," I said.

"I heard at the zoo there they have a two-headed snake," Jeff said. Right then I knew that he would make it to California and that I never would.

MILLIGRAMS

1. SUMMER

June and there's no A/C. The lobster we named Ralph crawls across Sasha's stomach. He has rubber bands on his claws. Sasha watches the ceiling fan revolve. Ralph nibbles at her belly button, runs a claw across her pubic hair. Sasha widens her legs. I take Ralph's claw, guide it over her clit. Ralph doesn't resist.

Sasha lifts her neck and stares at my face. I know she likes my full lips and my once-broken nose; they remind her of her father, she's mentioned, the one who almost touched her nipple but didn't, just moved his finger around it, which doesn't count as incest Sasha says.

Now Sasha's father pays the half of the rent that Andy's father stopped paying. He also pays for other stuff like lobsters and imported olive oil. If it *had* been incest, maybe he'd pay the whole rent, but I don't mention this to Sasha. She's still Daddy's girl, and one day soon I'm sure she'll call him and be gone from here, whisked away to Arizona or Malibu, to kind nurses and soft beds, softer than ours, which creaks and moans when we push against the springs, waking the neighbors and making us feel like rusty machinery, as if the sounds are being issued from our own bodies.

2. SNEAKERS

Sasha bought running shoes a couple months back. She's never worn them, but I think it's a sign. I imagine her in the white Nikes, heading west on the Pike. In this day-dream Sasha's legs are prostheses, the bionic kind given to the young vets I see on TV. The legs move of their own accord. Sasha's eyes are closed and she doesn't know she's running.

3. SUMMER

Sasha grabs Ralph by the claws. She lifts him into the air, holds him over us like a baby. I pinch her nipple, feel it harden between my fingers. Her ribs rise and fall beneath the weight of my hand. Sasha looks up at Ralph's under-side. He is squirming. She brings him down and places him between us on the bed.

"Are we gonna eat him later?" I say.

"I feel bad," she says.

"Do we have butter?"

"He gives such good head."

She one-beat stutter-laughs and then looks sad, as if

to say, "Ain't it funny, ain't it true, we all give head and then fall into boiling water." If we took off Ralph's rubber bands he'd pinch the shit out of us.

"Whatever," I say, and roll onto my stomach. I can feel Sasha sit up, and I know she's on the edge of the bed, leaning over the coffee table. I hear the crush and chop of her father's gold card. The ceiling fan whirs, but it's a quiet whir.

"We're out," Sasha says.

"Out of what?"

"It," she says, because she knows I don't say Oxy now that Andy's dead, I just say "it."

"Save me some," I say.

"We're out," she says.

4. LAST WINTER

The coffee shop was only selling coffee. No more sandwiches. No more croissants. No more dark-suited business types ordering extra foam. The only ones left were the junkies who stood out front jingling change and bumming cigarettes. They had nicknames, or no names, and part of me wanted to join their anonymous parade that marched the city at night, through the Chinatown gates, in and out of squats in the old Combat Zone, up Tremont to the North End, and out to the harbor.

Sasha wasn't one of them. You could tell from her haircut. Angles too precise, texture too full-bodied. She was from Connecticut—the good part.

5. CALIFORNIA

Ralph's in a pot of boiling water and the apartment smells like the ocean, which I haven't seen since my parents loved me, when they spent big bucks and sent me to Malibu Horizon to become a different person, the kind who goes to college and brings home girlfriends for Thanksgiving.

When I say my parents loved me, I'm pretty sure I mean it. Money is the truest form of love. If I had money I'd buy eighty milligrams. My parents think that's the opposite of love—self-hate, they used to say, self-destruction. How to explain that for some of us love comes out of our bodies, and for others it's something we have to put in?

Malibu Horizon cost them a chunk, and they never forgave me when I came back East and back to the way I was before. I wasn't ready to be an adult, an ex, a former. I'm not sure I am now, but I think about it some nights when Sasha's sweat feels like glue and I can hear the machine lifting the dumpster outside McDonald's and dropping it.

6. DINNER

Sasha stands at the counter chopping parsley and pretending that we're real people. She's wearing jeans and she doesn't have a butt anymore, or never did. Her half-blond hair is long and tangled. It covers her back like a dirty poncho.

Ralph is dead. I got a stick of butter from the store. I bought white wine too. It's not what I want, and the lobster's not either. I want to call Mike and have him come over, but Sasha doesn't get money until the first, and the first isn't until Monday. Mike doesn't take credit cards. Sasha's father put a cap on cash-back from her Amex. In the meantime we have Ralph and the rest of my paycheck, which can't get eighty milligrams, not even forty. There were no dollars in the tip jar, just nickels, dimes, and a Canadian quarter.

"Do we have any weed?" I say.

"Maybe," Sasha says, and then repeats a line from the radio, which plays songs she thinks are old because she was born in '86, but that I remember from high school— *"Jesus don't want me for a sunbeam."*

"Where would it be if we had some?" I say.

"I think I finished it when you were at work," she says.

"Maybe J. Smooth has something," I say.

"He doesn't," she says. "I saw him yesterday. He doesn't."

"Maybe he got some since then."

"Call him," she says.

Ralph's done. The parsley butter's in a coffee mug that says Busch Gardens. It must have been Andy's. I take Ralph's steaming body, crack it open with my hands, lick his juice from my fingers. "I wish we had those small forks," Sasha says.

In bed, post-Ralph, Sasha tries to get me hard with her hand. It's not working. Her hands are dry and she's pulling too forcefully. I encircle her wrist with my thumb and forefinger, pull her hand away. I can't sleep. Sasha moans while she gets herself off. Her breath is grasping, as if she's trying to recall a song heard in a dream; the words are on the tip of her tongue.

7. HOW WE MET

I'd been watching her for days: her straw-fiddling, her chapped-lip-cracked blood-dripping. She read a book and sometimes the sections of day-old newspaper that lay scattered across the tables. I liked the idea of the newspaper, thought of myself as the type of person who would read a newspaper.

Outside she bummed a cigarette.

"Hey," she said. I nodded, leaned back against the brick wall. It was like a movie. A bad movie that you watch because you want your life to be like it. Sasha didn't look like the girl in the movie. Her teeth were too big and her hair wasn't blond enough. She stared across the street at a cute kid walking his dog.

"I hate kids," she said.

"Fuck 'em," I said. It was lucky I didn't have a kid. It was lucky I had a bed and it was nearby. It was lucky Andy was dead. Not for him, but for the purposes of my sex life. His dad still paid half the rent.

8. GUESTS

I wake up to someone banging on the door. My logic: it's got to be J. Smooth; he must have drugs. I put on jeans and don't bother to button them.

Two guys. One is Alex Sammerstein, Andy's brother. The other is Dennis Gundy from the grade above me.

"Come in," I say. I lead them to the plaid street-couch that has holes and what I sometimes call "character" when Sasha complains, waves her gold card.

Dennis and Alex don't sit. Dennis leans against the wall and raps it with his knuckle. Alex pans the apartment, assessing the ripped *Big Lebowski* poster; the single photo of our old dog Papi held to the fridge by a magnet that says "fortuitous," a leftover from a disappeared set of poetry magnets; Ralph's crushed shell, which lies in the sink.

"Long time," he says.

"Yeah," I say. "Whatup."

"Whatup," Dennis says.

9. THEN

Dennis was scrawny, with a ponytail and sideburns. He wore tie-dye and never got laid, one of those guys whose friends are slightly better-looking and more confident. He probably wrote poems, threw them away.

Alex once lay down in the middle of his street and told me he wanted to be flattened by his mother's SUV, for her to back out and see his broken body, see the bones she grew in her womb destroyed under the weight of her car. He had the same look you see in sci-fi movies when an alien is using someone's body as a shell. Andy and I had to drag him back into the garage.

10. NOW

Dennis has cleaned up—his shoulders are broad, his hair hangs just above his ears, his sideburns are trimmed, his clothes are mixed prep with a touch of hip-kid slim—and he probably went to college, has a job, and is self-sufficient with slight parental assistance. His posture has improved, though he still stands with outward-facing feet.

Alex, I know, is at Suffolk Law and doesn't smoke pot anymore, which is weird because he gave me my first joint, first hit of acid, first pill of E, and first hand job—which he didn't actually give me himself, but convinced Sheryl Yung to give me because she was drunk and I was an adorable freshman. I'm sure he hates me now, holds me responsible. It wasn't my fault, though; Andy wanted to die high, said it constantly. Alex never came by. He never peeked in and said Andy's name in the firm tone of tough love.

"You still have Andy's shit?" Alex says.

"What shit?" I say.

"His shit," Alex says.

I'm not sure what he's talking about, but it doesn't matter because Sasha walks out of our room in a white terry-cloth bathrobe she stole from a hotel we rented on Virginia Beach in January with her dad's card. We'd holed up in it for days looking at the beach from our window. This was shortly after Andy died, when Sasha and I were new and sick of winter.

Alex and Dennis look at her. She's not so beautiful. And now she's bony with dirty hair. But still, something in her gaze must penetrate. Her chapped lips squirm into a half-smile that is both disconcerting and dick-suck-offering.

"We have guests," she says to no one in particular.

"This is Sasha," I say.

"Yo," Dennis says, and then blushes because he's still shy around girls even now that he's in skinny jeans.

Alex is staring at the photo of Papi on the fridge and fig-uring out that he's dead. The apartment doesn't smell like dog, hasn't for a long time. It was Andy's fault, not mine.

Or it was both our fault. We wanted to be dog people.

"Where's the dog?" he says.

"Heaven," I say.

"Who are you guys?" Sasha says. She's standing on one leg in a yoga position that she sometimes stands in when she wants to emanate calm. Her right leg is bent and tucked against the inner thigh of her left. You can see her bare leg almost up to her crotch, where a swath of robe hangs loosely. Her hands are held in prayer position in front of her chest. Dennis looks at her, then looks away.

"Alex is Andy's brother," I say. I wonder why she looks so calm, if it's because she's hoarding and hiding, getting high in the bathroom when I'm not around. She's not fidgeting and tongue-biting like me.

"Oh," she says, and puts her leg down.

11. ANDY

We don't talk about Andy. I met her a month after he died. His door stays shut, though I see it when I pass to the kitchen or the bathroom, and I know Sasha does too. Once Sasha said we should turn that room into something, a guest room, and I said yeah, one of these days.

"Where's all his stuff?" Alex says.

"Like what?" I say. "I don't know what's his."

"DVDs," he says. "DVD player. Laptop. Bike."

"He didn't have a bike," I say.

"He had a bike," Alex says.

"He didn't have it here," I say, though now I remember the bike, an orange bike that stayed in the closet for months until Andy sold it.

"Whatever's his is in his room," I say.

12. ANDY'S ROOM

There are large clumps of lint in the corners and stuck to the pillow, but other than that it still looks like someone lives here. His cell phone's plugged in and it says "charge complete." The sheet is half off the mattress, and you can see where someone drew a heart onto the foam and wrote "MB+LS 4 Eva."

Alex kneels and picks up a DVD—no case, just the disc. The DVD is mine, and I'd forgotten I owned it.

"Andy loved this movie," Alex says, and I say yeah and sit on the mattress, which isn't where I found Andy.

Dennis picks up a stack of CDs from the desk and puts them in a backpack. He doesn't look at them. Alex opens the closet and runs his finger across some hanging shirts. "There's not much here," he says.

Sasha stands in the hallway watching. She has her cell phone open but she's not talking. Alex lifts the TV and takes the DVD player out from under it.

"You don't want the TV?" I say.

"It's old," he says.

"I didn't sell it," I say.

Sasha has shut her cell phone and edged into the doorway, which she now blocks. Alex picks up a crumpled T-shirt from the floor, neatly folds it, then puts it back on the floor.

Dennis opens the drawers. There are a couple pipes, little glass ones. Dennis puts them in his pocket. He pulls out a bag of pot stems and places it on top of the bureau next to a pile of unopened junk mail and Andy's keys, which still have on their ring a rape whistle they gave out to girls in high school. Alex picks up a handful of pink Styrofoam balls from the floor and flicks them from his palm. Dennis pulls a prescription container out of another drawer and shakes it. There's no sound, and he places it next to the other items on top of the bureau.

"Where's his iPod?" Alex says.

13. THE BATHROOM

Alex grunts. "I'm a take a piss," he says. He'll see the wet magazines, the empty baggies and prescription bottles, the black mold, the red mold, the stray hairs, the beer cans, the loose pennies, the underwear, the T-shirts, the plastic bag filled with used tampons, the bits of dried mucus stuck to the sink bowl, the dried shit on the inside of the toilet bowl, the bloodstain on the tiles next to the toilet.

I don't care what he thinks. Maybe he thinks Andy's better off dead.

14. ALL YOU CAN EAT

Sasha sits on Andy's bed with her legs tucked and a lit cigarette in her mouth. She ashes into her palm.

Dennis looks at her, then looks at me. We used to be friends, used to eat all-you-can-eat Chin Ming Palace every Tuesday.

"How are you?" Dennis says in a voice that is meant to be compassionate, the way someone on TV might say it while staring at the ocean.

"Chillin'," I say.

"I'm gonna put on some music," Sasha says, but doesn't stand. Alex comes back into the room. He looks around.

"Pretty much it," Alex says.

"True," Dennis says.

"Den," I say, because that's what Andy used to call him.

"Peace," Dennis says.

15. DINNER

We don't do dinner. I sit at the table smoking cigarettes and Sasha watches TV in bed, something with a laugh track. I shouldn't have left Andy alone with all those milligrams, a scale of measurement that seems so small.

The thing is, I don't remember Andy's face, just his body, his legs hanging over the couch. He was wearing one shoe. On his other foot was a fresh white sock. He wanted to feel clean.

When the EMT came, he just said, "Shit." He was my age.

Sasha comes in during the commercial and stands in front of me in her bathrobe, one knee on the kitchen chair.

"Is there any food in the house?" she says.

"You talk to J. Smooth?"

"Yeah," she says. "No."

I don't know if she means yes or no.

"I'm starving," she says.

"There's cereal."

"Milk?"

"No milk."

We eat Apple Jacks and orange juice. It's not terrible.

"Do you love me?" Sasha says. What she's really asking is "Would you let me die?"

I nod.

Sasha digs her nails into my back and I want her to crack skin and draw blood. It's not that I want into her body so much as I want out of mine. I haven't come in weeks. Even with her teeth on my nipple it's hard to stay in the moment. I don't think about Andy, but I think about not thinking about Andy. I lose my hard-on and she goes to take a shower.

Andy, Papi, and Ralph are in heaven together. Andy rubs Ralph on some girl's clit, Erica Tanner's maybe. Erica had leukemia—the first from our class to be dead. She never liked Andy in life, but that was life.

Sasha comes out wearing a towel.

"We're out," I say. I think she stole Andy's iPod, sold it, got 160 milligrams, and put them up her nose when I wasn't around.

"Those guys who were here," she starts to say, but then looks at me, touches my arm, and says, "You should call J. Smooth."

I think, *Are you fucking J. Smooth?*

"Tell me about Andy," she says, and I say, "He was."

16. THE FUTURE

I call J. Smooth and leave a message. "Jason," I say. "Jason." From now on I want us to have real names. I want to vote on Election Day. I want fresh milk in the fridge.

"Call me," I say.

17. HIGH SCHOOL

Jason Streich was the quarterback, and people liked him. Girls, I mean. People liked Andy and me, but it was different, a different kind of like. The point is, you can't blame high school, but you can't go back there either.

18. YOGA

We lie on the bed with the TV on, but I'm not watching and neither is Sasha. She's doing yoga, what she calls bed yoga, which isn't really yoga, just stretching in bed. I know her body well enough to know it isn't mine.

"Andy's iPod," I say.

She doesn't say, "What iPod?"

Who gives a shit about the iPod? It's probably in a drawer.

19. ANDY'S ROOM

"Sometimes I go in Andy's room," Sasha says.

20. THE WEATHER

The doorbell rings. Jason, wet from rain.

"It's raining," Sasha says.

21. FEET

On the couch, Sasha in the middle. Jason takes off his shoes. His feet are bare; his shoes are slippers. There's black hair on his toes. Sasha rubs his feet.

We play music that we know is right. We've seen it in movies, seen the strobe-light stutter and time lapse. Sasha leans her head into Jason's lap.

I think: three bodies are not two. I think: three bodies are all ones. I think: she'll fuck J. Smooth as soon as I pass out. Sasha lays her legs across my thighs. Her toenails are overgrown. They are dead skin. How can something grow if it is dead?

ACKNOWLEDGMENTS

I'd like to thank the many editors who massaged these stories over the years, some gently, others less so: Kevin Allardice, Peyton Burgess, Jackie Corley, Laura Isaacman, Sativa January, Kevin O'Cuinn, Minna Proctor, Derek Rubin, Randy Rosenthal, Rob Spillman, Lorin Stein, Sadie Stein, and Zack Zook.

I would also like to the members of my entourage: my agent, Erin Hosier, and my editor, Michael Signorelli. I always wanted an entourage.

These stories were written over a ten-year period, and it would be impossible to individually thank all the friends and colleagues whose input helped shape then, but a few stand out. One is my father, Jonathan Wilson, who never went easy on me. Nor was he prudish at the R-rated stuff, though he did once comment, "Dude, you are one weird dude." These stories would not exist without the many long phone calls during which we discussed them.

Another is my mother, Sharon Kaitz, whose clear-eyed, full-hearted worldview has indelibly colored my own, and who always knew when a story should end, usually about a paragraph earlier than I'd initially thought.

Sam Lipsyte taught me, by both example and encouragement, to embrace the darkness. Justin Taylor has been a superlative reader, amigo, and drinking companion. Paul Rome was forced, on many occasions, to listen as I recited nascent versions of these stories in my kitchen. He never once complained.

I'd also like to thank my grandmother, Charlotte Kaitz, for allowing me to use her house in the Berkshires as a private writer's retreat. Many of these stories were written there.

Finally, I would like to thank Sarah Rapp, who not only provided invaluable insights into each and every one of these stories, but who also made sure I got out of bed every morning and left the apartment on occasion. Sarah never let me succumb to debilitating defeatism. Instead she made me laugh and smile. Without her there would be no book.

BOOKS BY ADAM WILSON

FLATSCREEN
A Novel

Available in Paperback and eBook

Flatscreen tells the story of Eli Schwartz as he endures the loss of his home, the indifference of his parents, the success of his older brother, and the cruel and frequent dismissal of the opposite sex. He is a loser par excellence who struggles to become a new person in a world where nothing is new. Into this scene of apathy rolls Seymour J. Kahn. Former star of the small screen and current paraplegic sex addict, Kahn has purchased Eli's old family home. The two begin a dangerous friendship, one that distracts from their circumstances but speeds their descent into utter debasement and, inevitably, YouTube stardom. By story's end, through unlikely acts of courage and kindness, roles will be reversed, reputations resurrected, and charges (hopefully) dropped.

WHAT'S IMPORTANT IS FEELING
Stories

Available in Paperback and eBook

Bankers prowl Brooklyn bars on the eve of the stock market crash. A debate over Young Elvis versus Vegas Elvis turns existential. Detoxing junkies use a live lobster to spice up their love life. And in the title story, selected for *Best American Short Stories 2012*, two film school buddies working on a doomed project are left sizing up their own talent, hoping to come out on top—but fearing they won't. *In What's Important Is Feeling*, Adam Wilson follows the through-line of contemporary coming-of-age from the ravings of teenage lust to the staggering loneliness of proto-adulthood with a delicate balance of comedy and compassion, lyricism and unsparing straightforwardness.

"Delivers rapid-fire prose that is distinctively intelligent, hilarious, artful, and perverse . . . stealthily exposes the psychic abyss that haunts every fit of laughter." —Heidi Julavits

Visit HarperCollins.com for more information about your favorite HarperCollins books and authors.

Available wherever books are sold.